THE BETRAYAL WITHIN

ERNEST MORRIS

GOOD 2 GO PUBLISHING

The Betrayal Within
Written by Ernest Morris
Cover Design: Davida Baldwin, Odd Ball Designs
Typesetter: Mychea
ISBN: 9781947340602
Copyright © 2020 Good2Go Publishing
Published 2020 by Good2Go Publishing
7311 W. Glass Lane • Laveen, AZ 85339
www.good2gopublishing.com
https://twitter.com/good2gobooks
G2G@good2gopublishing.com
www.facebook.com/good2gopublishing
www.instagram.com/good2gopublishing

PROLOGUE

IT WAS MONDAY AFTERNOON, and I only had fifteen minutes left before I had to be at work. I was sitting on my bunk reading a book called Forbidden Passion by Ernest Morris. My bunkie was getting his snacks together that he was going to take to work with him. We both worked as inmate porters in the Medical Department at the prison. I was serving a mild sentence for being stupid. I thought I had my life together, but of course I was so wrong. Now I was paying the ultimate price for it, my freedom.

"Yo, Stud, you ready to roll out, bro?" I asked, putting the book down and grabbing my tablet.

"Yeah, I was waiting on you," he replied.

"We out then!"

I walked over to the officer's desk and picked up the clipboard with the tracking sheet attached to it, and then signed both of our names to it. The officer pulled out two passes, filling them out with our names, numbers, and so forth, and passed them to me. I playfully snatched them out of her hand. She gave me this look as if to say, No the fuck you didn't." I smiled.

"Enjoy the rest of your day, and I'll see you tomorrow," I told her.

Officer Wynette Hayman was from the Scranton area. Actually, she lived down the street from me. In her uniform, her body was tight, so just imagine what she looked like when she wasn't in her work outfit. At five foot nine, with light skin, and 135 pounds, she was by far one of the baddest officers there. She had one child that she spoiled rotten. Her baby's father was doing time in a federal prison, but she was riding with him.

When he was first sentenced, he told her that he loved her and that she shouldn't wait on him. He knew that that hole between her legs would need special attention from time to time and he would be unavailable for a while. Even if she did creep with another man, her body and soul would always belong to him. He was the first man that she really ever loved.

"No you won't. I'm off tomorrow."

"Okay. well have fun for me." I winked at her, and she knew exactly what I was referring to.

"You better stop playing before I write your ass up."

"You could never write me up. You know we here," I said, waving two fingers from my eyes to hers. "Besides, you love me too much."

"Moore, get your ass out of here and go to work before I fuck you up," she replied, shaking her head.

That was the kind of friendship we had. We would talk shit to each other. We knew when, and who we could say it around. Me and Stud headed over to work. When we got there, we placed our passes in the slots with our names on it and did our normal routine, which consisted of filling the water containers, sweeping and mopping, putting the laundry away, wiping everything down, etc. Once we finished all those things, our main concern was taking care of Brawny. He was what we call a one-on-one because he needed 24/7 care. He suffered from a rare form of dementia.

As we sat at the table with a couple of the other workers, Cherry walked in with a new nurse following behind her. She was the second shift supervisor and our boss. She spoke to the officer, then stopped in front of us.

"Everyone, this is our new nurse. Chelsey, these are our hardworking porters, well some of them," she joked, looking at Stud. "No, but seriously, these guys make our jobs so much easier. and they're really good with the patients."

"Hi, guys, nice to meet you," she said, giving off this erotic aura that Cherry quickly picked up on.

"I see I'ma have to keep my eyes on you." Cherry smiled, playfully nudging her.

"No, none of these guys are my type," Chelsey replied, her eyes never leaving mine.

I never paid it any attention, but Stud and Howell did. They looked at each other and smiled. Cherry escorted her into the nurses' station to introduce her to the rest of the staff.

"She looks like she's gonna be a problem," Harris said.

"Why you say that?"

"She just seems like the you-can't-tell-me-nothing type," he said.

"I think you're reading too far into it. You just assume that she's going to be a bitch before you even get the chance to know her," I told him. "Besides, you don't have to deal with her, traitor. Remember, you left us for the morning shift."

"I only left because I can't stand that fucking lady."

"Who?" Stud asked.

"Ms. K. We never did get along. She irks my soul," Harris replied.

Harris used to work on our shift until he quit just so he could move to the morning shift. He used different excuses as to why he left, but I later found out the real reason. He wanted to be on the same shift that the head of the Medical Department was on. He ran to her about everything. Ms. Hart was the CHCA (certified healthcare administrator) of the prison. Anything that had something to do with medical had to go through her first.

Harris was her eyes and ears, but in a good way. I think she did an extraordinary job though. Anything you needed, as long as it wasn't something we knew we couldn't have, she would do what she could to get it for us. I was glad that she was the big boss.

"She never did nothing to me. Maybe I have to see what everyone else is seeing."

"Yeah, bro, 'cause you blind to shit. We try to tell you something and you don't want to listen to us," Stud said in an irritating tone.

"That's because I try not to judge prematurely. I used to do that and was wrong most of the time. Now I try to at least give people the benefit of doubt until they prove me wrong."

Stud's problem with Ms. K was more than that though.

She tried to get him in trouble on some bogus shit. She told her supervisor that he was hitting on a patient. That almost got him sent to the hole. Luckily our regular guard was there that day and knew that it was bullshit. Stud still had to go through all the questioning and other shit before a final decision was made though.

From that moment on, he despised the ground she walked on and wouldn't say anything to her. After finishing up with the introductions, Cherry and Chelsey came back out of the nurses' station and headed back up to Cherry's office. She needed to talk to Chelsey some more before she started shadowing one of the nurses for a couple of hours. Chelsey had this swagger about her. She walked with so much confidence that you would think she ran the place. It made me momentarily wonder if maybe Harris was right about her.

Little did I know that this was the calm before the storm. What went down in the next few months not only changed my perspective on people, but it also made me understand how quickly a person could go from being liked, to being hated.

Also in that time, I saw a lot of things that I wasn't supposed to see and heard shit that I was never supposed to hear. Confidentiality was out the door when it came to being in prison, and I would get a taste of it firsthand.

ONE

"IF YOU NEED HELP with anything, I'll be floating back and forth in the area," Brad said, leaving the nurses' station.

Chelsey was the infirmary nurse today. She had trained for two days, and now she finally had been left on her own. Her experience came from her time as a trauma nurse. She said she had been doing it for almost ten years, but I found that hard to believe since she was only twenty-five years old. That meant she would have started when she was fifteen. Maybe she was taking one of those classes in high school where they do intern work for credits toward college. Look at me once again justifying someone's story. When it came to her, I admit I was kind of biased. That's because I liked her. Shit, there were a few women here that I had a thing for. I knew she was a staff member, and there was no fraternizing with staff, but the vibe I got from her in the last couple of days said so much more. The one thing I did know was, no matter what kind of vibe I got from any of them, I was smart enough not to even think about acting on it, especially not in this place. Maybe once I left here, because then no one could tell me what to do.

"I will let you know," Chelsey replied, as she got ready to do her three o'clock insulin lines. As I was wiping down the door handles and light switches, I saw Penelope coming down the hall. Cherry and Ms. Hart were gone all day because they had to do training in Harrisburg. That left Penelope as the team leader because of seniority. She walked into the infirmary moving fast as she always did, grabbed some papers, and headed into the back office to make some calls. She needed to find someone to come in for the ten to six shift tonight. One of the nurses had called out. "Hey, Renata, this is Penelope. Are you able to work ten to six tonight?" she asked.

"Sorry, but you know I don't do over time," Renata replied.

That was the truth. Since she been working there, Renata only did overtime a handful of times. It wasn't that she didn't need the money. She just hated working around certain people. "Thank you anyway," Penelope told her, then ended the call.

She tried the next person, and the next person, but still got the same results. Either they were too busy or already had something planned. Nine calls and eight denials later, Pene-lope finally found someone to cover the shift. Karen, who mostly worked in the pharmacy, took the shift. The only time she didn't have to work in the pharmacy was when she worked overnight.

"Okay and thank you. I thought I was going to be stuck here tonight if I didn't find anyone," Penelope said.

"I find it so crazy that everyone is always crying about overtime, but when you ask them to work, it's always some lame-ass excuse," Karen told her.

"What you expect? I asked Cherry if I could add a person, so Jamie will be staying for a half shift to help out also. She's leaving at two."

"Well let me go. I have to make dinner for my husband before I leave."

No sooner had Penelope hung up the phone than there was a medical 55. She rushed out of the office and into the nurses' station to grab the response bag. Brad was just coming back from RHU and joined in to assist her. One of the other porters had already pulled the stretcher out for them so they could just take off running. Chelsey felt antsy as she watched them run down the hall. I was upstairs cleaning. A patient in the parole outpatient clinic went back to his block, so I had to get the room ready for the next one. When I came back downstairs, Chelsey was on her way to the bathroom for the umpteenth time since she arrived. We figured she was in there vaping as usual, but who knows what she was really doing. My mind went straight to the gutter once again. "Damn, she going to play with herself again?" I smirked. Everyone laughed, even the two guards standing there.

She was only in there for a minute or two, but it seemed like she was in there forever. Me and Stud made a bet to see how many times she would go in there for the whole day. Howard and Peacock also wanted in on the bet. When she came out, you could tell that she had been doing something. Peacock was a big-time drug addict, so he swore she was doing drugs. We knew damn well that wasn't true, or else she wouldn't be working in here. She walked back toward the nurses' station, then stopped in front of us. We were about to play a game of cards with one of the patients.

"What kind of cards are y'all playing?"

"Pinochle," I answered. "You know how to play?"

"No, you will have to show me one day when it ain't so busy."

"I got you!" She went back in the office and sat down.

A few minutes later, Jamie came from next door carrying two cases of diapers.

She was a CNA and was very good at her job. She

worked in the afternoon, and Jimbo, who was also a CNA, worked the morning shift. The rest of the medical staff was lucky to have them around because they both helped out so much and took a lot of the weight off their shoulders. There was one patient that no one wanted to change. Every time he shitted, you knew what to expect. It would be everywhere. When he released his bowels, it looked like someone had poured a pot of soup all over the place. The smell alone could make the toughest person puke up everything they ate that day. It seemed like he was admitted to the hospital every month. I'm not gonna lie, I think the man was sent from heaven to test our patience or willpower. He was more needy than a woman. Every two minutes, he was calling one of the nurses for something. When they came, all he wanted was to be tucked in, or something stupid like that.

"Um, Chelsey, I think Mush just shitted," Peacock said. "He has that whole room stinking."

"Well I can't do anything right now, so he's gonna have

to wait," she stated.

The only thing she was doing was sitting on the computer. Peacock walked away shaking his head. At that moment, Jamie was just finishing up with what she was doing.

"Ms. Jamie, Mush shitted. Peacock said something to Chelsey, but she said she couldn't leave out of there right now," I said.

Jamie didn't respond. She just shook her head, grabbed a pair of gloves, and walked into the room. I put on some gloves also because I wasn't going to let her change his fat ass by herself. Soon as she removed the blanket off of him, it looked like a shit show, *literally*. He had shit everywhere. It went all the way up his back and down his legs. Even his hand was covered in it.

"Mush, what the fuck?" I said to him.

"I tried to call somebody," he lied.

"No you didn't. We were all sitting right there, so don't lie."

"I did," he kept saying. Jamie went to get the shower chair while I started throwing all the soiled linen in the garbage. It was too messed up to save. Harris came in to help out. Me and him helped Mush up into the chair, while Jamie held it so it wouldn't move. While she gave him a shower, we remade his bed. Chelsey finally came in to help out, but it was already too late. We had done everything.

"Sorry, guys, I was trying to get here sooner," she said, putting her gloves on. "Jamie, do you need any help?"

"No, we're done," she replied, drying Mush off. I could tell that she really wanted to say, "Bitch, where were you when I was washing all this shit off of him?" But she kept her composure and did her job. That was one of the things that I

liked about Jamie. She was willing to get down and dirty. She didn't mind changing diapers, or getting the patients water, because that's how she passed the time away. The only thing I didn't like is when people tried to take advantage of her, whether it was the staff or the patients.

"Okay, stand up and hold the bar so I can get underneath you," Jamie told him. Mush stood up, and there was still a bunch of shit on his ass. Jamie wiped him clean and put on the new diaper.

After getting him back to the bed and laying him down, I went back over to finish playing cards. Just like that, Chelsey made her way back to the bathroom.

"There she go again," Peacock said. We just laughed. Stud was dealing the cards and tried to tuck something under his arm without anyone seeing it, but got caught.

The CO Hurts started laughing. "Hey, what you got under your arm?" We all looked in Stud's direction. He smiled and pulled the cards out. It was five aces. He gathered up the cards and reshuffled them.

"Damn, Hurts, I di . . . di . . .didn't think anybody se . . . . se . . . seen me."

"I was looking right at you, wondering what you were doing. I thought Moore seen you too."

"Don't worry, I'm watching his ass now," I told Hurts.

They had just announced that count was clear over the PA system, so we stopped playing cards. It was time to get back to work. Howard walked Brawny while we cleaned up. Harris left so he could get some rest for work tomorrow. Everything looked like it was going smoothly, but that was far from the truth when dealing with the infirmary

.

TWO

"*SO WE LOST ANOTHER* patient?" Dan asked, walking into the nurses' station, noticing that the patient's door across from them was closed and the blinds had been drawn.

It was 5:45 a.m., and they were switching shifts. Dan was the regular infirmary nurse for first shift. The patient he was referring to was Mr. Salters. He had been locked up for a very long time for murder. The crazy part about it was he wasn't the one who actually committed the crime. It was his brother. Salters decided to take the charge because his brother had a family and he didn't. He was also in Camp Hill for the riot back in the '90s. He saved a couple of staff members' lives by pulling them into his cell and hiding them. Even though it was a nice thing to do, I don't think that I could do life for a crime I didn't commit.

"Yes, he died a few minutes ago," Tiny said. She was one of the ten to six nurses who attended to him in his final moments in this world. Tiny was around five foot five and 127 pounds, with short brownish-gold hair that was always in a ponytail, and a smile that could melt ice cream. She was very polite, but if you pissed her off, she could be a real bitch. I never saw her that way, so I can't cosign it. Then there was Ms. H, Ms. D, and Ms. N. They were the dream team of third shift, who alternated working each night. You would have at least two of the four there no matter what.

"What time are the coroner and state police coming to pick the body up?"

"We called, and they should be here between seven and

eight. I did all the paperwork they need. Dino already signed it when he came in. You ready to count the narcotics and syringes so I can get out of here?"

"Yeah, yeah, let's go do that," Dan replied. He was peeking through the blinds. Once they finish counting the equipment, Tiny and the rest of the night workers headed out to the sally port.

All the other nurses came in, and each stopped to see Salter's body still lying in the bed. Sliver, Harris, Tyler, and Lang were feeding all the patients while Jungle started cleaning. There were two patients that were in the room with Salters, and Harris and Lang brought them out and sat them at the table.

"So I wonder who's the next to go?" Mary questioned.

"I hope it's that fat piece of shit right there," Joanie replied, looking at Mush. "He's like a cockroach that just won't die. He's gonna outlive all of us." Everyone sitting in the office laughed.

As soon as they saw Dino come down the stairs, they began scattering like cockroaches. So who's really the roach? Kris headed over to K2, Joanie headed back to the pharmacy because they had to do the morning meds, and Dan got ready to do his morning insulin. They were already running behind because the officer didn't want any inmates coming over to the infirmary while the body was still there, but that was something they couldn't stop. People needed their medication. Dino walked past the nurses' station and headed back to talk to Helena, who was the infection control nurse for the prison. Anything that dealt with a disease of any type, they had to deal with her. People didn't like her because she thought she knew everything and thought she was everyone's boss. There were other reasons, but I would be all day trying to share them. They talked for a few minutes, then Dino headed back up to his office to get some paperwork done. As he walked by, he spoke to the porters. "Hey, guys, how's it going?"

"Good morning," they all replied in unison. "If y'all need to speak with anyone about Mr. Salters, let me know. It's sad, but at least he's in a better place now." He continued upstairs, leaving the workers to finish doing what they were doing.

~ ~ ~

"Hey!"

"What's going on?"

"I have a couple of hours before I have to be at work. Are you busy right now?"

"Well, I just got finished cleaning up. What did you have in mind?"

"One thing. Can I come over there, or would you like to come here?"

"Well you know you can't come here because she's home. I tell you this, I'm going to take a quick shower and put my work clothes on 'cause I also work today. Then I'll come over to your place. Can you give me about a half to get there?"

"Okay, but hurry. I need a stress reliever." Chelsey ended the call and took a pull of her vape. She walked over to her hamper and pulled out her jeans that she wore to work the day before, then grabbed a shirt out of the drawer. After getting her work clothes together, she sat on her bed with only her panties and bra on, watching Maury. Not even a half hour later there was a knock at her door. She didn't bother covering up because she already knew who it was. She opened the door and smiled. "Hey. I've been waiting on you," she said, walking away from the door, giving him a full view of her ass. He immediately got turned on at the sight of the white laced thong she was wearing. He stepped in, closing the door behind him, and followed her into the bedroom. There were no more words spoken as he quickly got undressed and sat on the edge of the bed. Chelsey kneeled down in front of him and wrapped her hand around the length of his girth. He closed his eyes, anticipating what was next. She stroked it up and down with her hand a couple of times, making sure that it was nice and stiff. With her tongue, she licked the tip, causing him to let out a soft moan. Her mouth was hot and wet as her head slowly went up and down on his penis. It felt so good that he grabbed the back of her head, pushing it down further, causing her to gag a little. Chelsey was very good at giving head, and she knew it. The feeling was so good that he tried to pull away from her.

"Where you going?" she asked, standing to her feet.

He just smiled.

"Do you trust me?"

"What kind of rhetorical question is that? Do I trust you?" he said, looking at her strangely. "Why are you asking me that?"

"Just answer the question."

"To a certain point, why?"

Chelsey didn't answer him. She straddled his lap. Lifting up just a little bit, she reached for his penis. He tried to say something, but she put a finger over his lips. Chelsey pulled her thong to the side and positioned his erection with her now moist vagina. She slid down, taking all of it, then started rotating her body on it. The feeling had him ready to explode. She could feel him tensing up and started moving wildly. Suddenly, he realized the mistake he was making. Just as he was shooting his load, he pulled out.

"Why did you pull out?"

"What you mean? I'm not wearing a condom. You're not trapping me up like that," he said.

"When I asked you if you trusted me, that's what I was talking about. I wouldn't jam you up. I'm on the pill," she told him, standing up. She pulled off her thong and got back on the bed. "We still have an hour to play with if you're still in the mood."

He couldn't resist the beautiful sight of her pussy. Already knowing that he was about to feast on her goodies, she stuck a finger inside, then stuck it in his mouth. "You taste like strawberries," he said, spreading her legs and diving in headfirst. The feeling of his tongue hitting her G-spot had her body shaking in a matter of minutes. He wasn't done yet though. As he continued eating her out, he stuck a finger inside her asshole. Between his tongue in her pussy and his finger in her ass, Chelsey exploded three more times. After letting her get off, he was ready to get another one off himself. He climbed on top of her, positioned his penis, and slid inside her once again without using a condom. The heat radiating from her pussy was breathtaking.

"Damn this is good," he said, breathing heavy. He tried to kiss her, but she wasn't having it.

"I told you no kissing, just fucking," she moaned back, opening her legs even wider.

That was part of their agreement. Whenever they met up, it was strictly for sex—no kissing. Chelsey felt like kissing was too intimate, and she didn't know him well enough to have feelings. She didn't know any of the men she had been having sex with. The only thing she knew about them was they worked at the same prison she was working at. Since she started working there, she had sexed a few. As much as she tried to keep it confidential, it still leaked out to other staff members in some kind of way. Even some of the inmates, like me, knew what was going on. She just hoped her boyfriend didn't find out. He was a part-time EMT. She hardly saw him due to his job being far away, which caused her to stray. Her appetite for sex was at an all-time high. Especially since she worked around men all day long. While at work, she couldn't wait to leave to get one off.

"My bad," was the only thing he was able to get out, because he was on the brink of releasing his load again. He pre-ejaculated inside her. When he pulled out, Chelsey knew exactly what to do. When he stood up, she grabbed his manhood and placed it in her mouth, sucking ferociously. In the blink of an eye, he was ejaculating down her throat. She swallowed everything. She ran her tongue over the tip of his dick, making him tense up from the feeling. "Oh shiiiittt," he yelled, trying to move back, but she held onto him so he couldn't move. Chelsey was a pro when it came to oral sex. When she lived out in Baltimore, she used to be a phone sex operator. She would sit home watching pornos, collecting ideas. One day when she was in the house alone, she pulled out her ten-inch dildo and practiced giving head. Once she had it down, she called over a friend to demonstrate on. She realized how good she was.

"I'll get you a soapy cloth to wipe off with," Chelsey told him, heading for the bathroom. After taking a quick shower and brushing her teeth, they headed to work. He took his car, and she followed behind in hers. They pulled in at different times so no one knew they were together. Little did she know, he had already been bragging about how good she was in bed to his fellow workers. They were just waiting for the right time to test the waters.

THREE

BECAUSE SHE HAD THE day off, Amie decided to clean the yard and wash her car. It was something that she had been prolonging for quite some time now. Since the sun was out and the humidity was high, it seemed like it was 86 degrees outside. She wore a pair of cutoff jeans and a T-shirt. The shorts fit her frame like a glove, and of course the T-shirt was tight. She wouldn't have it any other way. Her son came out to help cut down the branches and rake up the grass. It didn't take him long to complain about being tired.

"Mom, I'm tired."

"We've only been out here for an hour," Amie told him.

"I have to be somewhere. How about you wash your car, and I'll finish doing this when I get back?"

She told him to go do what he had to do, and she finished cleaning the yard by herself. After she was done, she started on her car. The humidity had her sweating profusely. It looked like someone had thrown a bucket of water on her, drenching her clothes. Luckily she was wearing a bra. The last thing she did after washing the car inside and out was shine up her tires and rims. By the time she was done, her Benz looked brand new. She opened up a car freshener and placed it inside, then went in the house to cook dinner. She hated cooking, so if she was going to cook anything, it was going to be her favorite meal. She loved lasagna. Once she prepared the meal and placed it in the oven, she went upstairs to take a shower. Since she was home alone, Amie decided to get comfortable and watch a movie on Netflix. She slipped into her pink teddy with the leopard ruffles at the bottom, and her leopard slippers to match. That was two of her favorite colors. She let her hair down and put on a little lipstick. You would have thought she was going out instead of staying at home. She fed her dog first, then made herself a plate of food with a glass of red wine.

"Well, looks like it's just me and you," she said to her

dog, who was chowing down on his food. "Let's see what we can watch." It was still early in the evening, and Amie had nothing to do. She ate her lasagna and watched a couple of movies before drifting off to sleep. She woke around nine o'clock to the sound of moaning. When she opened her eyes, she noticed that it was coming from the television. A couple was having sex in the pool. As Amie watched the couple go at it, she started getting turned on. She didn't know if it was the wine, the fact that she hadn't had any in a while, or a combination of both. Her hand mysteriously made its way under her teddy, inside her panties. It was soaking wet. There was a tingling sensation every time she touched her clit. "Mmmmm," she moaned. Her eyes were now closed as her finger caressed her forbidden area. The scene was over, but she wasn't. She grabbed her cellphone and logged into Pornhub.com. It didn't matter which one she watched, as long as she got one off. It only took five minutes before she was releasing her juices inside her panties. She pulled them off and continued playing with herself. After having a couple more orgasms, she went into the bathroom to wash up. Amie felt drained once she finished cleaning up. She threw on a long T-shirt, without any panties, and got into bed. She was out within minutes of her head hitting the pillow.

~ ~ ~

The Medical Department was packed today when I arrived at work. There were so many inmates there for different reasons. They were waiting in the waiting room to see a physician. I spoke to the morning shift, then started getting ice water and filling up the cup dispenser. By time I was done with that, the rest of the porters that worked the same shift walked in. Howell started walking Brawny up and down the hallway, while I put the laundry away.

"You need any help?" Peacock asked.

"I'm good, thanks," I told him as I continued fixing the messed-up sheets on the shelf so that I could put the new ones up. Around 1:45 p.m., second-shift staff started pouring in. Jamie, Cherry, and Brad walked back to the break room to hang up their jackets. Seconds later, Jimbo came out of the room from changing a patient and went back to meet Jamie to give her the keys and let her know what was going on for the day. Cherry came out of the break room first. "Good afternoon, boss lady," I joked.

"Good afternoon," she replied, stopping at the door. She walked into the closet where I was and looked around at how neat everything looked. "It looks really good in here. You did this by yourself?"

"Yeah! I didn't want any help. I just wanted to zone out and get it done. Hopefully it'll stay this way, even if it's only for a while."

"Well, you did a good job."

"Thank you! It's nice to be complimented on the fine work that I do in this place," I said sarcastically.

Cherry laughed and walked away, stopping at the nurses' station to talk to Dan. His relief still hadn't gotten there yet. He told her about the couple of patients that needed to be one-on-ones because they were unable to care for themselves. Cherry told him that she had already sent an email to the doctors and was waiting for a response. Dan's relief finally arrived a couple minutes later, just beating the two o'clock mark. Any later, and she would have been late. Technically, she wasn't really late, but it was a mind game. Burnout Barbie came in switching like always, thinking she was on some kind of runway, and started counting the syringes and other things. All the porters shook their heads when they saw who was in the infirmary for the day. Once she was done, Dan grabbed his jacket and walked out of the nurses' station. Burnout Barbie sat at the desk and began getting her insulin stuff ready.

"Oh fuck," Peacock mumbled.

Peacock and Burnout Barbie, whose real name was Sissy, had words before. One of the patients who was supposed to get Ativan every night wasn't getting it. He kept trying to tell her, but she took it the wrong way and thought that he was trying to tell her how to do her job. She told him to do his job, not hers. As much as he wanted to say something back, he didn't, out of fear of going to the RHU with a write-up. He had no outside support at all, so this job was his lifeline and he couldn't mess it up. He did the right thing by keeping his mouth shut and simply staying away from her.

"I'ma ask Ms. Cherry to make sure she gives him his right medicine tonight," Stud said as they all stood around watching them talk inside the office. "These people are crazy."

"I rather have Chelsey here. How she get a day off already?" Howell asked.

"They probably got her somewhere else today," replied Peacock.

As soon as Cherry came out of the office, Stud pulled her to the side to talk. She said she would say something to her when she came back down, then headed up to her office. The first thing they all thought was that it wasn't going to happen because that was her friend. As they were talking back and forth, I walked up. I was done with the closet and was about to sit down to join in on the conversation. I heard a little of it, but not the whole thing from the beginning.

"You don't have to ask her about it. I'll say something to Ms. Sissy later," I said. "Sometimes you just have to know how to talk to them."

"W-w-we already tried," Stud started. "You haven't been down here long enough to see that these people don't care about shit. Big bro, I watched them do crazy shit to people." I couldn't argue with him because he was right. I hadn't been working here long enough to see everything that went on behind the scenes. All I could do was comment on what I knew, and that wasn't that much.

"I'm just going to ask politely. If it doesn't work, oh well." Stud gave me this crazy look as if he wanted to say something slick but chose not to. We had a brotherly relationship. If he did something wrong, I would check him on it, and I hoped that it would be vice versa. There are things that we agree to disagree on, but that's life.

Around four o'clock, after serving dinner and cleaning up, we sat at the table to play pinochle. This is what we did every day when we took our break. It would be Stud and Peacock against me and a patient named Dom.

As we played cards, Jamie came out to check Brawny. "Is Brawny wet?" she asked, putting on a pair of gloves.

"I got him," Howell said, coming out one of the rooms. We pulled out the table, and he took him into the bathroom to get changed. After Jamie was done changing Brawny, she walked over to K1 to check on a couple of other patients. She liked to make sure everyone was dry before she took her break. There was something about Jamie though. She wasn't like some of the other nurses. You know how some people come to work, do their eight hours, then go home? Well, when Jamie came to work, it was to really take care of the patients. She cared more than you would expect her to. That was one of the things that had me infatuated with her. I would do anything to make sure she was safe in this volatile industry. Don't get me wrong, there were other nurses here who took pride in caring for patients. But you also had the ones who didn't give a fuck who lived or died. To some, we were the scum of the earth because we were in prison. But in all reality, they were just one DUI or worse away from being in the same place. Everyone in prison is not a complete asshole. Some people just made careless mistakes and now are owning it. For the most part, we are just trying to get back home to our families. I can't speak for everyone else, but I miss my little girls and they miss their father.

FOUR

COUNT HAD CLEARED, AND they were calling blocks to mainline. Since I was on the work line list, I usually went whenever they started calling the other blocks. As I was coming back from the chow hall there was this guy walking down the hall near the auditorium. Suddenly he collapsed, falling headfirst to the ground. He wasn't moving. The south corridor officer witnessed the scene and immediately called the medical 55 over his radio. It took less than two minutes for medical to arrive on the scene. RN Stevie Bender began performing CPR on the inmate. The officer told everyone that was standing around to move back down the hall, but I could still see everything from where I stood. He looked like he was already gone before the stretcher arrived. Two officers helped another nurse load him on the gurney while Steve continued doing chest compressions. By law, once you start doing CPR on someone, you can never stop until they are revived or pronounced dead by a doctor or physician.

"Let's get him back to the infirmary," Steve said, sitting on top of the inmate, continuing to do CPR.

As soon as they got him in the ten to six room, they finally pronounced him deceased. The nurse covered his face with a sheet.

"Time of death, 11:51 a.m.," the doctor said before walking out of the room.

"I'll call control and let them know," Sgt. JC said, dialing on the cordless. He talked to the shift commander for a few minutes, giving him the inmate's ID number, then ended the call. "State police and the coroner are on their way."

"Thanks, Steve, for trying to bring him back," MJ said as they sat in the nurses' station afterward trying to catch their breath from running.

"We were just doing our job."

"Maybe if we would have gotten there earlier, the

results could have been different."

"No, he died before he hit the ground," Steve told her.

"I know, but I still wish we could have saved him," MJ replied.

"Fuck him. He was a child molester anyway. He needed to die," an officer walking by said. He was on his way to K1 and heard them talking.

"That's not nice," Marry said.

"It wasn't nice when he was molesting those little girls either. God did us all a favor." You could see the anger all over the officer's face as he spoke. He took shit like that real serious. I'm not going to lie, when I found out what that dude was in for, I felt the same way. We all have our own opinions about things, and I know only God can judge, but stuff like that eats at my skin. All the women out there that love having sex, and people choose to do that to children? You deserve to burn in hell for that.

"Jess called a few minutes ago when all the commotion was going on and said the doctor cleared Johnson to go back to his block," Tara told the infirmary officer.

"Yeah, well, it's still a shit show in this place right now, so he might not be going back till after shift change."

"Hey, whatever you want. I was just telling you she spoke defensively."

"Jimbo, Tiana said that the supplies you were supposed to pick up from the warehouse, you can get them tomorrow instead."

"Oh, okay," Jimbo replied.

Since it was getting close to quitting time, he walked in the room to check Brawny and Mush. To his surprise they were both still dry, so he went over to K block to mess with the officer. The state police and coroner still hadn't arrived to pick up the body yet. Officer Will locked the door to the ten to six room until they decided to show up. Around two, his relief came in to take over. He told him everything that was going on, and officer Hurts shook his head in disbelief. Nothing surprised him about the prison anymore. Just like everyone else, he expected the unexpected. He checked his equipment and called it in to control, then went about his normal routine for the day.

"What's up, Hurts?" I said as he walked by doing his start-of-shift count.

"What's up?"

"You see the surprise in the room down there?"

"Yeah I seen it! Control just called and said that they're here now. They're waiting for the Area 4 sergeant to come escort them up."

When they came for the body, Officer Hurts started doing extra stuff, trying to impress his superiors. Me and Stud looked at each other and laughed. We both were thinking the same thing. They placed the body on the stretcher, then covered him with a sheet and black blanket. As they pulled him down the hallway toward the elevator, Howell walked ahead of them to hold the door open. Penelope and Cherry were standing by Richie's office talking when Amie came out of the pharmacy and headed down to the RHU to give out the early meds. She was wearing her black scrubs and her regular cherry-red lipstick, looking like the superstar she knew she was. As she walked past M1, there were inmates coming out to go to the gym. To a person that had never seen her walk before, it would've seemed like she started switching even harder as they walked behind her. But that was the way she walked. It was like she was always on the runway modeling.

"Damn, her ass is fat," one of the three inmates said. "Every time I'm trying to catch her walking by, I be too late. This must be my birthday gift from God."

Amie heard him but didn't respond. She just laughed knowing that she made someone's day, even though she wasn't trying to. They followed slowly behind her until she went inside the RHU door, and then they went about their business.

"Hey," Amie said, speaking to the officers who were standing there. "Are you going to be my escort?"

"I got her," the sergeant replied, walking up from behind

them. He walked her to the six cells that needed their meds, and then they stayed in the back for a few minutes and talked. Like every other guard in the building, he had a crush on her.

"So when you going to let me take you out?"

Amie smiled.

"I'm serious. I just want to take you out to eat or something. We'll go wherever you want to go."

"I don't know. I'm busy with school, and whenever I'm not doing that, I'm working."

"We'll make time then," he smirked.

Amie smiled back and started heading toward the door. He tried to squeeze her ass, but she smacked his hand away. She was used to getting attention from inmates and staff, but now she was starting to get it even more from married men. Yeah, the sergeant that was hitting on her was married with kids. "I have to get back to start Medline," was her only response before walking out. As she headed back down the hallway, of course there were more inmates going in the same direction. She heard all the little comments they were making, but wasn't paying any attention to them. As soon as she walked through the red doors, inmates were sitting in the waiting room. Officer Hurts was sitting in the ten to six room emailing our time sheets to the business office. "I'm ready when you are," Amie said, heading inside the pharmacy.

"Okay, here I come," he replied. He finished up with the email and then logged off and left the office to get the line started.

FIVE

CHELSEY SAT IN THE nurses' station logging in her ACU checks. Peacock was standing by the door, when he decided to strike up a conversation with her. He made sure no one was in there with her, or watching them before making his move. "Chelsey, I have a question for you," he said, leaning on the counter.

"What's up?" she asked, giving him her undivided attention.

"You get medical marijuana, right?"

At first she gave him a weird look, but then she nodded her head yes. She was trying to see where he was going with that question. "How much of it can you get at one time, and what else can you get?"

"I think you need to walk away from here asking those types of questions. Now!" Peacock stood there at first, smiling. Once he saw that she wasn't smiling back, he walked away from the counter and sat at the table with everyone else. We were just talking and acting stupid with the patients. No one even noticed the look on Chelsey's face when she walked past, heading to her favorite destination. When she came back, though, she motioned for me to come over to the nurses' station. I got up and followed behind her.

"What's wrong?" I asked, noticing that she looked mad about something.

"You need to talk to your coworker. He's asking me inappropriate questions, and if he asks me something like that again, I'm going to let Cherry know."

"Who? Peacock?"

She nodded.

"What did he ask you?"

"Things that he shouldn't. That's all I'm gonna say, and if it ever happens again, he's gonna be in trouble."

"I'm about to check his ass right now," I said, smirking as I walked away. I could tell whatever he said to her, hit a spot. She looked like she wanted to cry. That was the first time I'd seen her tear up, but it was far from the last. I pulled Peacock to the side so we could talk. "Yo, what did you say to her, 'cause she's pissed?"

"I just asked her how she got her medical marijuana pass."

"You sure that's all you asked her?"

"Yeah, why?" he lied.

"Because she's ready to get you out of here. You can't be asking people shit like that, bro. What, you trying to get her to bring you something in?"

"No, I didn't ask her nothing like that!"

"Yo, you can't even lie with a straight face. You trying to get back into your dope fiend ways. Don't be asking her no shit like that. She's only a temp. You trying to make her lose her job before they can even consider hiring her."

When it was all said and done, Peacock had this dumb look on his face. I walked away from him and went back to doing what I was doing. I really didn't know him, but I knew this wouldn't be the last time we had an altercation.

~ ~ ~

Later on that day when Officer Wat came in, shit got crazy. He was sitting down at his podium doing his work before he had to call medical treatment. For some reason, I guess he wasn't moving fast enough for Chelsey's taste, so she yelled down to him three times. He ignored her. Then suddenly he picked up his phone and called the nurses' station. Soon as she answered the phone, Wat went off on her.

"Who the fuck you think you talking to? Don't be fucking yelling at me. When I'm done, I'll let you know." He hung up in her ear before she could respond.

Chelsey sat at her desk, tears running down her face, and just stared at the computer screen. Stud was about to ask her something, but when he saw the look on her face, he walked away. She put her head down so no one could see her.

"Yo, my nigga, she in there crying," Stud said when he came back over to the table. We all looked in the direction of the office. Sure enough, you could see that she was going through something. "I-I-I th-th-think p-p-pops cursed her out for rushing him."

"Damn, she is," I replied, walking over to the window. "Hey, you okay?"

"Yeah, what's up?" she said, looking in my direction.

"I just wanted to make sure you were okay, that's all. You know I'm here for you if you need someone to talk to."

"Thanks." I felt sorry for her because everyone was picking on her. The fact of the matter was, she needed to grow some balls and push back or she'd never make it in this business. Once they saw that they could walk over you, they'd continue to do so until they pushed you out the door, making you quit. If you thought the staff was bad, wait until the inmates saw that they could get over. She really wouldn't last long. A few minutes later, the captain was making his rounds and stopped at the nurses' station like he usually did when he came through.

Chelsey told him what happened earlier. He told her that he would say something to him, then walked away. Me and Stud stood by the wall as the two of them talked for a few minutes. The only thing we heard Officer Wat say was, "I don't care about her feelings. I'm here to do my job." It shocked me that he was talking to his superior like that. Then it dawned on me, he was only saying that because this was his last week. He was retiring on Friday. They talked briefly for a few more minutes, and then the captain headed over to L block. I could tell that Wat wanted to yell at her some more, but he took the high road and bit his tongue. When he saw Chelsey walking back to the break room, he followed behind her. They were back there for at least ten minutes talking. Once they came out, you could see the look of relief on her face. Later she told me that he apologized to her and gave her a hug. She said she felt like a little girl in his arms, being embraced by her father after having a bad dream. That was something I would have had to be there to see in order to believe it. Wat didn't give a damn about anything except his cousin Amie.

And even that wasn't true half the time. When I first got interviewed for the infirmary job, he told me that most people only wanted to work here just to see her. Then he said everyone liked the way she strutted around the place in her tight outfits, displaying her assets for everyone to see. He said she was just an attention seeker and that a couple of staff members had already bedded her. I wondered why he was sharing that kind of personal information with me. Was it a test to see how I would respond? If I had said the wrong thing, I probably wouldn't be telling this story right now because I wouldn't have gotten the job. However, when I found out that they were related, I was appalled that he would talk bad about his own family like that. If he would do that to his own flesh and blood, I could imagine what he would say about other people.

SIX

KELLS WAS SCHEDULED FOR the pharmacy today, so she had to distribute medication to the RHU unit. When she walked through the doors, Officer Tiece was waiting for her. He escorted her around so she could give out the meds to the inmates. Some of them were whistling and making noises, while others made sly remarks as she passed by.

"Don't wait for me to walk past to talk shit. Say it to my face," she said as she tried to see who was talking reckless to her.

"Fuck you, bitch," one inmate said, and then ducked down so she couldn't see him.

"Suck my dick," another one yelled.

"Alright, knock it the fuck off before we extend your stay down here," Officer Tiece shouted, tired of hearing them being disrespectful to the nurse. The heckling continued until they were done doing meds. They didn't care about any extra time because half of them were already doing a shitload of time anyway.

Well, there was this one dude who only had about two days left in the hole. He decided that it would be a good idea to say something smart as Kells was about to leave. "I bet she got a good-ass shot. Look at how her ass jiggles."

Little did he know, Kells knew exactly where it was coming from. She turned around and walked right up to his cell. He damn near pissed in his pants when he heard the key turning in his door. When it opened up, there were two officers and a sergeant standing there. Kells made her way to the front. "Is there something you want to say to me now, you little piece of shit?"

"That wasn't me," he pleaded.

"Yes it was. Talk slick now," she said, gripping the little white kid up against the wall. By the time she was done with him, he was crying like a baby. The officers stood around, amazed at how she just handled herself. She walked out of the RHU with a smile on her face. Word got out around the prison fast.

"Hey, tough lady. I heard you made an inmate cry in the RHU," Officer Mat said when she returned to the infirmary. Mat was the K block rover. He was standing there talking to officer Hurts when she walked in.

Kells stood by the pharmacy door. "He was talking shit, and when I confronted him, he bitched up." They all started laughing. Only Kells knew the real reason the inmate bitched up. He saw all those guards standing behind her, and he wanted out of the hole. He had been there for almost six months on a thirty-day sanction for disruptive behavior. Now there was a chance that he might be doing more time if she gave the word to issue him another write-up. She accepted his apology and moved on. Kells wanted to be respected in the prison, and she wasn't going to take shit from anyone. If you let people push you over, they will do it. It wasn't going down like that with her.

"Who was the inmate?" Hurts asked.

"I don't know, some little skinny white kid."

"He probably was shitting bricks," Mat said.

"Well he picked the right one," she replied as she stepped inside the pharmacy to start her med lines.

~ ~ ~

"Peacock, you have to go take a urine," Hurts told him after he received a call from security. He didn't know what to do. Me and him was sitting in the room when Hurts gave him the message. Peacock got up and grabbed his shirt. The look he had on his face was priceless. He knew either way he was going to the hole, but he figured if he refused, he would only be in there for fifteen days. If he took the test and it came back positive, he would most likely get thirty to forty-five days.

"I'ma just refuse," he said.

I asked him if he was dirty.

"Yeah, I just popped last night. I knew something was going to happen when I saw them taking my man to the bucket. I think he snitched on me."

"Why the fuck would you be so stupid? You fucked up a good job and a great situation just to get high. Are you out of your fucking mind?" I snapped.

"I can't help it. Once an addict, always an addict. I'm real with myself. I just can't quit like most people. It is what it is."

"Man, that's the dumbest shit I ever heard you say. Change only can happen if you want it to. If you want to be a junkie for the rest of your life, then that's exactly what you're gonna be. You have to want it more than anything else."

"You ready?" Officer Hurts said.

Peacock nodded.

"Here's your pass."

"Good luck, man," I mumbled, knowing that he wasn't coming back. I couldn't believe that he risked everything just for some pills. He really was a fiend. Me, Stud, and Howell had a deep conversation about life and continuing to do the right thing when we got our chances to go back out into society. I just hoped that we all followed through with the plan.

About two hours later, an officer was walking past with a cart containing Peacock's property. As he headed toward the RHU, Penelope was walking by in a hurry. She always walked fast wherever she was going. The officer tried to ask her a question, but she ignored him. She was mad about something and didn't want to be bothered. She walked into the nurses' station and sat down.

"What's wrong?" Renata asked.

"Chelsey was supposed to work today and didn't even call or show up. Now I'm the one running around trying to do every goddamn thing. I don't know how she still has a job. Every weekend she calls off like she's entitled to those days off."

Renata listened on as Penelope vented her frustration of the past couple of hours. Many of the workers were starting to have problems with Chelsey's behavior. It was just a matter of time before shit hit the fan. She was just about to go to lunch when a lockup came over the radio. Penelope stood up, grabbed her equipment, and left to meet them.

SEVEN

AROUND TEN O'CLOCK SHIFT was changing, and all the two to ten staff were exiting the building. As Officer Ly walked through the parking lot, he noticed a bit of commotion going on in the far right corner. As he got closer, he realized that it was two COs arguing about something. Minding his own business, he unlocked his car door and got in. When he started his engine and was about to pull out of the parking spot, he noticed a bunch of his fellow officers running toward the area where the two officers were just arguing. He could see one of the men lying on the ground, not moving. His first reaction was to jump out and help, thinking that he needed medical assistance. Then he saw two officers pulling the other away from the man on the ground.

"Damn, did he just knock his ass out?" Ly mumbled to himself as he drove off. Before he got home, he stopped at the Sheets gas station in Dickson City to fill up his tank.

When he walked inside to pay the cashier, this half-decent woman stood in line in front of him waiting to pay for her food. From behind, she looked gorgeous and had a body that made any man's dick jump to attention. Her face was average, and she had enormous breasts.

"Can I help the next person in line?" The cashier smiled.

The lady stepped forward, and so did Ly.

"And can I get a pack of Newport 100s please," the lady asked, sitting her food on the counter and then reaching into her purse for her debit card.

"You can put her order with mine," Ly said.

"That's not necessary. I can pay for my own stuff."

"I know that, but it wouldn't be fair if I let someone as beautiful as you pay for their own stuff. Besides, it's only $12."

"Well thank you," she said, then smiled. As soon as Ly looked inside her mouth, he wanted to puke right there. Her teeth were rotten, and half of them were missing. He closed his eyes.

"Hey, I said thank you."

"My bad, you're welcome," Ly replied, opening his eyes. They walked out of the store, and Ly headed over to pump the gas in his car. The woman headed toward her own vehicle, which was a 2020 cherry-red Corvette. When he saw what she was driving, he suddenly had a change of heart. "What is your plans for the next hour or so?"

She looked up and smiled. "You if I'm lucky." That was all he needed to hear. Ten minutes later they both were in the backseat of Ly's SUV, and she had her head in his lap giving him the best blow job he ever had. He'd never gotten head from a woman with no teeth before. Her gums felt like he was inside her vagina. The sensation had him erupting in her mouth in a matter of minutes. Once he was finished, he went home to his wife and kid. She was lying on the couch watching the evening news when he walked in. He spoke and headed straight to the bathroom to wash up. She never suspected a thing. Before Ly left, he gave the woman his info and told her to hit him up. He wanted to see what she was all about.

~ ~ ~

"So I just read the email you sent me. Are you sure that's exactly what you saw?"

"Yes, I stood right there and watched her do it. That is the reason I'm coming to you."

"Okay," Ms. Hart said, picking up her phone and dialing a number. "Can you come down to my office real quick? We have a bit of a situation."

A few minutes later, Lt. Edmond from the Intelligence Unit knocked on the door and walked in. He was in charge of security for the facility. His true job was basically the head of the Gang Unit. He knew shit about people that no one else knew. A lot of his information came from the many informants he had floating around throughout the prison. They would tell on their own momma just to get some extra commissary.

"So tell him exactly what you saw."

Karen had been asked to come in a half hour before her shift started so that she could speak with her boss and the Intelligence Unit about something she saw one of her coworkers doing. For the next fifteen minutes, she told the security lieutenant what she witnessed. He recorded their whole conversation. Once they were done, Lt. Edmond left Hart's office and radioed his security team to call him. "We have a situation. Meet me in my office."

"On our way, Lieutenant."

The security team was just switching up with first shift when they got the call. After receiving instructions from their lieutenant, they headed down to the infirmary. They found the person they were looking for and asked her to come with them up to the office to talk. Even though she looked dumbfounded, she knew what it was for. She let the other nurse know that she would be back in a few minutes and was escorted by a lieutenant, sergeant, and two regular COs up the stairs. I was standing there when the whole thing went down. I really thought that she was about to get escorted out of the building, but that didn't happen. Later on I found out the reason why they took her up to the security office, and it surprised me that her own friend would tell on her. In my head, I thought, if she would tell on another staff member, then what would she do to an inmate? Karen said she saw this nurse placing pills into her pocket. She also witnessed her taking pill packs inside the bathroom and coming out empty-handed. This information sparked an immediate investigation. She wasn't allowed to work in the infirmary until they completed their investigation and cleared her name. Instead, she was reassigned to work on the K units. She was pissed about it at first. "If they try to walk me out of here, I'ma knock that bitch out on my way out the door." It'd been a while since I'd seen a chick fight, so you know I was stoked to see something pop off. That would have been awesome.

EIGHT

"HEY, YOU," AMIE SAID, peeking inside the ten to six room. "Are you over here today?"

"That would be correct," Sgt. Mann replied, looking at her as she entered the room.

"Good, cause I'm in the infirmary today. I'll be there all night until 2:30 in the morning. I'm staying for Tiny."

"I thought we were going to hang out tonight."

"Can we do it tomorrow night when we're both off?" Amie asked, giving him this puppy-dog look. That had him feeling turned on in so many ways. Sgt. Mann stood up and pulled her over to the back, out of sight from the door. He lifted her up on the counter with ease and stood between her legs. She placed her arms around his neck and kissed him. Mann stuck a hand between her legs, rubbing her pussy through her pants. She was wearing tights under her scrubs like always, but he still could feel her getting wet. Amie started moaning as she continued to kiss him. Stud walked in to ask Sgt. Mann something. When he saw the two of them entwined, he backed out of the room quietly and went back to work.

Me and Howell were talking to one of the patients, when Stud came in and told us what he saw. "Yo, I j-j-just saw Amie and the sergeant k-k-k-kissing in the room." Neither of us said anything. We stood there waiting to see them come out. Inside the room, Amie and Mann had heard the footsteps and stopped, thinking that it was a white shirt. They walked out of the office.

"Meet me downstairs when you go on break. Since you have to work late, I was thinking that maybe me and you could enjoy lunch alone. You have something that I want to feast on." Amie smiled, knowing what he was referring to. She agreed to meet him and then went into the nurses' station to get her work done before break time. She didn't play around like she usually would do. She was done by 3:30.

"You ready?" Sgt. Mann asked. He had just come off of

K block checking on his officer.

"I'll be right there," Amie replied. She was waiting on her relief to come from C2. Just as the words were leaving her lips, Renata was walking down the hallway. She passed her the keys and took off behind Mann. They went down the back stairs and into the dentist office. They left the lights off because what they were about to do, they didn't need to see anything. Amie quickly removed her pants and tights and then sat on the examination table. Sgt. Mann kneeled down between her legs, pulled her panties to the side, and inserted his tongue into her vagina. The sensation hit her instantly. She leaned back until her back was against the wall and arched her hips so she was getting full penetration from his warm tongue. "Mmmmm, that feels so good," she moaned.

Sgt. Mann wasn't the best at oral sex, but he played his part. He kept sucking and licking her clit until he thought she was about to cum. Sensing her body tensing up, he stood up and pulled down his pants. Amie started rubbing his dick to make sure he was hard. He was definitely lacking in that department, and they both knew it.

"Stand up and bend over the table," he ordered. She did what she was told, spreading her legs apart in the process. Sgt. Mann entered her from behind and began pumping slowly in and out of her. Amie was so wet that his dick kept slipping out. He slid it back in and pumped a few more times before it popped out again.

"Oh my God, you're so big," she lied, trying to boost his ego. In fact, Sgt. Mann was only about five inches fully erect. He was only able to get a few more strokes in before he felt his nuts tensing up. He pulled out just in time to shoot his load all over her ass cheeks. Amie reached back and smeared it all over and then stuck her fingers in her mouth. She then turned around and sucked the rest off his penis, leaving nothing.

"Control to the area 4 sergeant."

"Damn, we finished just in time." Sgt. Mann started grabbing his radio. "Area 4, go head."

"2516."

"10-4." By the time he responded to his call, Amie already had her pants back on and was ready to leave. He made sure his own clothes were fixed and they left the dental office. They walked back upstairs and went into the staff break room. Amie took her and Sgt. Mann's Gatorade out the refrigerator and then they left. As they walked out, Cherry was coming. "Where were you? I was looking all over for you."

"I walked out to my car," Amie said, quick with a response.

Cherry knew she was lying, but since she couldn't prove it, she took her word for it. Sgt. Mann headed over to the L and M blocks, leaving them to talk. Amie kept thinking that she was forgetting something, but didn't know what. Jamie came out of the office to change Mush, and Kate came along to help so they could hurry up. They were about to have a meeting.

"We'll talk later," Cherry said as they stepped into the

office. Suddenly Amie realized what she had forgotten. Before they left, they didn't wipe up the evidence they left behind in the dentist office. All it would take was for one of the dental staff to come in to work tomorrow and see semen all over the table and floor. That would spark up another investigation. As soon as the meeting was over and she had a chance to leave, she hurried back downstairs and cleaned up what all the staff called the "boom boom room."

NINE

2019 WENT BY SUPER fast. Before we knew it, it was 2020, and the world we knew suddenly took a turn for the worst. There was a new virus called the coronavirus (COVID-19) that was invading our country. It had already claimed lives all over the world, and the death toll was rising at an all-time high. People were beginning to panic, thinking that it was an act of war by the Russians. I was talking to Ms. Hart that afternoon before she left for the weekend and told her that she should think about having some workers over to live just in case we got locked down. She said that she would have to look into it. The problem was finding somewhere to put us. We had suggested the dayroom, but she didn't want to use it because that was where the inmates waited to be seen by the doctor or other medical staff. There really wasn't anywhere else that we could make our living quarters besides the dayroom, or that space out in the open where the table was. I didn't know about anyone else, but if they said that's where we would have to sleep, I wasn't coming. You would have no privacy, and it would definitely be loud as hell from the staff walking back and forth through there. I guess all we could do was trust the process.

"Let me get back to you on that," Ms. Hart said. "That is a good idea. I just have to talk to the deputy and see if we can put it in motion. Don't worry, I'm listening to everything you said."

"Okay, thank you. I'ma let you get out of here now. Have a good night and drive safely."

"You do the same. Good night, guys. See you on Monday," she said, waving bye to everyone as she headed out the door. We kept asking the guards if they thought we would be getting locked down because of this virus taking over, and they couldn't give us a straight answer. The only thing we could do was wait and see how bad this virus got.

"I can't wait to get out of here next week," Howell said. He had been paroled and was now waiting to leave. It couldn't have come at a better time for him either. A couple of weeks ago, he received terrible news about his son. When he told me, I couldn't believe it. We did everything we could to comfort him and make sure he was okay. Even the nursing staff gave him words of wisdom. I could tell that some of them really cared. Even Chelsey had something good to say. She was a good person when she wanted to be.

"Just make sure you hit us up when you get home, and don't forget about us," Stud told him.

"I could never forget about you. I'm gonna send you some money," Howell said. He then looked at me before I could say anything. "I ain't sending you shit. You don't need nothing."

"Okay!"

We all sat around joking a little longer, and then me and Stud went back to the block. Since it was his last week working, Howell said that he would stay late every day until he had to pack up.

~ ~ ~

Monday morning they made the call for count. After the officer finished counting, I did my normal morning routine of making my bed, going to the bathroom to brush my teeth, and washing my face. I sat on my bunk watching television until count cleared. As soon as control cleared the count, the lieutenant got on the intercom, informing us that the facility was now on a modified lockdown. I knew it was going to happen, I just didn't know when.

"Damn, bro, looks like we won't be attending our hospice class today," I said to Stud.

He had just woken up when he heard them on the loudspeaker. "I wonder if they gonna call us over to work."

"Man, we gonna be bored as shit."

"I should ask the guard to call over and see if they gonna have workers over there."

"Fuck it, if they need us, they'll call here. We sat around

all day waiting for them to call us to work, but they never did. When second shift came on and the rover came through, I asked him about checking to see if they needed us. He told me that they already had workers over there. That pissed me off because I thought that Harris had done some sneaky shit behind our backs and just got the morning shift workers over there. Since I was going to be stuck on the block, I went into the dayroom to play cards. For the next couple of days, all I did was gamble or watch television if I wasn't finishing my book *Forbidden Passion*. I only wrote that book because an officer asked me to. Wednesday around 5:00 p.m., I had just finished washing clothes and was on my way back to my cube, when Cherry, Stud, and the sergeant were standing there waiting on me.

"So you two didn't want to come over to work, huh?" She was pretending like she was mad.

"We tried to get over there, but they said they already had the workers they needed."

"Yeah, whatever. Come here," she said.

I walked over to her and she took my temperature.

"Pack up your stuff, you're coming over. When you're done, let the officer know so he can call the area 4 sergeant."

"I'll be back to get you," the sergeant said. Him and Cherry left the block. Everybody was telling me that I shouldn't go because someone in the prison contracted the virus and they were probably over there. Of course I paid them no attention. Soon as I was done packing up, the block officer was about to call the area 4 sergeant, but the L&M rover was there, so he walked me over. Harris had already made my bed and everything for me. I unpacked my stuff and sat in the room for a while talking. He told me why they didn't call us over when we first went into lockdown. I told him that we had to get Stud over here with us.

When I came out, Amie was walking out of the pharmacy. "I see you made it over."

"Yes, I'm here now."

"Good." She headed out to do her RHU meds.

I was looking for Chelsey but she was off today. The new nurse was in the infirmary. Kimmy had started working in February. She was one of the few RNs that they had. Renata was on K2, and Kay was working on K1. For the rest of the day, I got myself accustomed to being housed in the infirmary. It seemed like it was going to be fun being over there instead of on the block. Little did I know that this would be the start of seeing all the drama firsthand that these nurses went through every day. From laughing in each other's faces, to the talking about each other when they weren't around, this is what happens when you put a bunch of women together. Some of them hate on each other.

TEN

CHELSEY WOKE UP IN the morning with a slight headache. She couldn't even remember what she had done the night before. All she knew was that she was lying in the bed naked. She looked around the room trying to see whose house she was at, but nothing looked familiar to her. There was a video playing on the 55-inch flatscreen television that hung from the wall. She glanced at the screen for a moment and then reached for her pounding head. Chelsey's eyes got wide as she looked back at the TV screen. There was a man and two females engaged in all kinds of foreplay. She didn't recognize the man and the other female, but one did stick out: it was her. She was between the woman's legs giving her the best head of her life, while the man was behind her with his head buried inside her ass.

"Oh my God, what have I done?" she said horrified, looking around to see if she saw any cameras. There was nothing in sight. She grabbed her clothes off the nightstand but couldn't find her panties. She would have to do without them. Just as she slid on her skirt, she heard the toilet flush.

The bathroom door opened, and the female from the video stepped out wearing nothing but her panties and bra. "I see you finally woke up. My boyfriend went out to get us breakfast if you're hungry," she said, picking up the half dutch that was sitting on the table next to some pills. She lit it and took a couple of pulls. "Want some?"

Chelsey shook her head no. The chick took a couple more pulls and then put it out. She walked over and sat on the bed next to Chelsey. She started playing with her hair. Chelsey moved slightly away from her. "What did we do last night?"

"What do you mean? It's obvious we had a good time," the female said, pointing to the TV screen. "That was all your idea. You wanted to party and release some stress. You said you hated your boyfriend."

Chelsey continued to watch the homemade video they made. The more she watched, the more it was beginning to turn her on again. She had to cross her legs to keep her juices from escaping. The female could tell what was happening by her body language. "What did I take? My head is killing me."

"We smoked some weed and took some E pills, and then you said you wanted to show your boyfriend what he was missing. You then took out your phone and started recording me and my man making out. You wanted to join in, so he pulled out his phone that was connected to our television, and we got it in girl."

"Why would I say I wanted to show him what he was missing?" Chelsey asked, still not understanding what was going on.

"Apparently he's some kind of paramedic or something, and you were talking to him on the phone. Y'all had this heated conversation about him being so far away, and then you hung up and started kicking it with us."

Chelsey tried to remember last night, but it was still a bit fuzzy. She did remember the conversation she had with her boyfriend though. Matter of fact, she had decided to have a couple of drinks with her coworker after work, but there was a problem with the babysitter, and she had to get home to her son. Chelsey decided to go alone.

"So we met at the bar?"

"Yup! You started flirting with my boyfriend, and I said if you wanted him, then you had to have me too. You gave me this look, and before I could get another word out, your tongue was down my throat."

"Damn, I guess you think I'm some kind of freaky bitch, huh?" Chelsey grinned.

"No, I think you're a woman that knows what she wants and is not afraid to go after it. There's nothing wrong with exploring your sexual inhibitions. I wish I had the heart you got, girl."

Chelsey was grinning from ear to ear. "Shit, you got me in your bed last night."

"That was all your doing. Those two E pills mixed with the drinks had your kitty cat on fire."

That had both women laughing. They were laughing so hard that they didn't see Gary standing in the doorway with two bags of food. "Do I want to know what you two are laughing at?"

"We were just talking about how she ended up in our bed last night," Amber said, looking at the bag with the food in it. "Let me get my food. I'm hungry."

"Me too," Chelsey said.

Gary sat the food down, and they all started eating. He went to turn off the video they made, but Chelsy stopped him. She asked Amber if she had some more of the E pills she had last night. Amber pointed to the table. Chelsey popped two of them and then took her pants back off. Gary and Amber looked at each other, then back to Chelsey, who was now fingering herself. She stuck two, then three fingers inside her pussy. You could hear it making all kinds of squishy noises.

"Are you gonna watch, or help?" she said to the couple. That was all they needed to hear. Gary was out of his clothes before Amber could come out of the bra and panties she was wearing.

They enjoyed their sexcapade for about two hours before Chelsey realized she had to leave to get ready for work. After she put her dress back on, she turned around and smiled at the couple. "Thanks for last night, I needed that. Oh, by the way, if you find my panties, keep them as a token of my appreciation." Chelsey walked out, closing the door behind her.

ELEVEN

PENELOPE WAS SITTING IN the nurses' station chatting with a few of her coworkers. It was their downtime before they had to get back to work. Since this pandemic had hit, they hardly had any time to breath. Their jobs had gotten much harder now because they had to go to each block to deliver meds. Amie, Jamie, and Renata were the other people in the room with her.

"It's time to go eat," Penelope said as she stood up to leave. As they continued talking, Chelsey walked in all jolly. She sat on the trashcan and listened to what everyone else was talking about.

"What the hell is that smell?" Amie said looking around, as did everyone else. "Whatever it is, it's making me nauseous."

"I don't know what it is, but I smell it too," Penelope said, walking out of the nurses' station.

Even though they pretended like they didn't know

where the smell was coming from, it was obvious that they knew who it was. Chelsey got up and stormed out of the office with a look that could kill. She went down to Richie's office to be alone. I was dust mopping the floor, when I passed the office. She was sitting at the desk once again crying. After I finished sweeping, I put the dust mop up and stepped over to the door. Chelsey had her head down so no one could see the tears.

"Hey, you okay?" She looked up and saw me standing there. The half smile she gave me said it all. I knew something was wrong. I waited for her to get herself together before I pressed on.

She spoke before I said anything. "I'm just tired of these bitches picking on me 'cause I look better than them and their man wants to fuck me," she whispered. I was wondering what she was talking about. She must have sensed my confusion and continued. "I had to leave out of there because my perfume was making them sick. They're so stupid though. It's not perfume, it's my conditioner."

"Who did you make sick?"

"That big-titty bitch said she was feeling nauseous when I walked in. She just don't know that her man was trying to take me out the other day. I think I might do it."

"Listen, stop letting people get to you. You gotta stop being on the defensive side and go on offense. If they see you as a weakling, they will keep pressing. You have to have tight skin to work here, Chelsey. You think they're grinding you up? Wait till us inmates get a hold of you. This is a fucking prison and people will try to manipulate you any way possible."

"I'm just getting tired of all the bullshit that people keep saying about me. I feel like if they keep saying I'm doing all these things, then I might as well do it and give them something to really talk about."

"If you don't mind me asking, what things are you referring to?" I asked, trying to see if she would tell me.

"I don't really want to say," Chelsey said. I felt like she

wasn't gonna bite, and then she took the bait. "Brad telling people that I need to keep my legs closed, but he don't know who I fucked."

"Wow!"

"If my legs were always open, then they would be open now," she stated, stunning me. She turned her chair toward me and opened her legs as wide as they could go, giving me a view of her goodies. I just stood there and smiled to myself. "Now my legs are open, but ain't nobody in between them."

"You are crazy," I told her. "That's what I keep hearing. You haven't even seen crazy yet. Then this officer running around telling his friends that I come to work with no panties on. If that was true," she said, pulling the drawstring to her scrubs, then showing me the waistline of her panties, "I wouldn't have these on, right?"

I'm not going to lie, my dick jumped to attention when she showed me her red panties. I don't care what nobody says, I'm a man first, so you know I got excited. I had to look out the door to make sure the officer wasn't coming.

"I see you have a lot of frustration built up inside right now. It's not good to hold it in," I said playfully. That caused her to smile a little.

"No, I'm serious, Moore," Chelsey replied, fixing her clothes. "These people need to keep my name out of their mouths. Even the officers on C2 where I'm working today keep messing with me. I think Mat is only doing it to impress his friends. Wait till he try to text me."

"Loose lips sink ships. You need to tell them that and stop being such a baby. That crying shit is for the weak, and you don't seem like you're a weak individual to me. Maybe a bit emotional, but not weak."

"You know, you're not such a bad guy. If you wasn't in prison, I would give you a hug and kiss right now."

I smirked, but I didn't know about all that. This woman was crazy for real. If someone was in earshot of her talking like that, that would have caused some not-needed attention for both of us. Just from hearing and seeing how she acted toward the staff, I knew that she had problems. In fact, I thought that when her father was writing his psychiatric books, he was really writing about her. She needed to see a professional and check her mental status. "Just do me a favor and toughen up. They are going to drive you out of here if you keep letting them grind you up. I'm not going to tell you this again. Even if you have to do what I do and kill them with kindness. The reason I get the respect I get is because I give it even if people are dicks. I earned it, Chelsey, and so can you."

"Thanks, E, I mean, Moore," she said, calling me by my last name. She got up to leave the office. "I'm going to lunch and then back to my workstation. I'll be down here with you guys tomorrow."

"Remember what I told you and you'll be alright." I walked away as Chelsey came out and locked the door. By this time Officer Hurts had finished up what he was doing in the six to ten room. She walked over and started talking to him.

"Hey," he said when she sat down.

She began telling him what had happened to her earlier, but stopped so she could go grab something from the cafeteria. When she came back, the two of them finished their discussion. He basically told her the same thing I told her. Fight back, but not physically. For the rest of the day, Chelsey stayed away from the drama and did her job. Once she was done handing out meds, she returned to the infirmary with a chip on her shoulder. To avoid a confrontation, she sat back in the staff break room. Everyone else was in the nurse's station chilling. She never came out until it was time to leave.

TWELVE

OFFICER LINDS MADE HIS rounds and then stopped at the table where Lang was feeding Brawny. Harris and Sly were getting the trash ready, and I was in my bed asleep from working the overnight shift. Actually, I worked the afternoon and the overnight shift, so it kind of tired me out. It was fun though.

"What's going on, man?" Lang said.

"Same shit different toilet," Linds replied.

"How y'all like being down here so far?"

"I don't know," Sly said with some conviction in his tone. "I'm just doing my eight hours, and then I'm done. They can work long as they want."

"He thinks that we're not getting paid for the time we're working," Harris chimed in. "I guess he thinks we're working for free."

"You should get paid. They asked y'all to do them a favor. Who else gonna do everything that y'all do around here?"

"Well, when I see them get paid, then I'll work longer."

Linds started walking toward the back of the infirmary as Officer Ski was coming from K block. He smirked at him and playfully bumped Linds. Those two always played around with each other. It was all fun and games when it came to them. That was the way they passed their time. Ski was at the other end of the hall by the time Linds finished making his rounds. Suddenly his instincts kicked in, and Linds took off running back down the hallway. He didn't make it in time, and he received a call over the radio. It was control making sure he was okay. Ski had taken the phone off the hook, and when that happens, control gets an alert.

"Control to the infirmary officer, call 2505."

"You know I'ma get you back for this," he said, then pressed the button on his radio to respond to the call he received.

"10-4." After calling and confirming everything was

good, Linds wrote something down in the book and then started talking to one of the nurses that came back from one of the blocks.

"Now what did he do?" Jimbo asked.

"The same thing he always does. He took the phone off the hook again."

"You gotta get him back when he's on a block."

"That's going to be hard, because he's always the rover," Linds replied. He was about to say something else, but Harris called him. It seemed that one of the patients in Iso 2 was going through some kind of episode. He was trying to rip his skin with a stapler. Linds called for the area 4 sergeant, and then him and the infirmary nurse went inside the room to try to stop him from hurting himself.

"What are you doing?" Linds asked him. The inmate yelled something at Linds as he tried to charge him. Before anyone could blink, Linds had the inmate on the ground with his hands behind his back. Sgt. BC was just walking in when the whole thing went down. He called the 55 and rushed over to help his officer. All the commotion of the officers running through the infirmary woke me up. I didn't know what was going on until Harris came into the room and told me. Once the nurse checked him to make sure the cuts weren't life threatening, they strapped him up and took him up to the POC. We laughed at Ski as he grinded Linds up, saying that the inmate would have fucked him up if Sgt. BC hadn't walked in. Linds shook his head as he did his paperwork.

"I wanted to see that," I told Harris and Lang. They were standing there being nosey as usual.

"You didn't miss anything at all," Sly stated. "That guy is on some kind of medication and shouldn't have been down here."

"How you know?" Lang asked him.

"That's what they're talking about right now in the office." Sure enough, they were getting yelled at. Someone had fucked up, and Dino was letting them know about it. Jimbo came over and stood there with us. He told us how the inmate should have been in the POC getting treated instead of in a regular room, then left to go pick up supplies from the warehouse.

~ ~ ~

"Moore, can you give me a hand with this patient?" Chelsey asked. I stopped playing cards and walked over to the room to assist her with helping the patient get to the bathroom. He wasn't trying to walk, so we helped him into a shower chair, then rolled him in. As we waited for him to finish, Chelsey did something unexpected. She pretended like she dropped her ID on the floor and bent down to pick it up, giving me a clear view of the crack of her ass. At first, I didn't pay her any mind until she made a comment about the floor being sticky.

"I'm going to clean the bathroom in a few minutes," I told her, turning around just in time to see what she was doing. My eyes almost popped out of my head when I noticed she wasn't wearing any panties.

"Are you done?" she asked the patient. He nodded his head. "Okay, you have to stand up so I can wipe you, okay?"

I grabbed the wipes and passed them to her. As she grabbed the pack, she purposely rubbed her index finger over the back of my hand. If I didn't get the hint before, I damn sure was starting to get it now. I needed to be sure though. "On three, we're going to lift him up," she told me. "One, two, three." We helped the patient up, with me taking the bulk of his weight, while Chelsey wiped him clean. After she finished and put a new pull-up on, together we sat him back down in the wheelchair. We pushed him over to his bed and helped him lie down. In the midst of it, Chelsey's ass brushed my hand. To my surprise, it was really soft.

"Excuse me," I said, trying to be respectful.

"You didn't do anything. That was on me." She gave me a wink before walking out of the room. I was stunned by her sudden boldness. I knew she was flirtatious, but what she was doing was borderline PREA status. She wasn't going to get me jammed up. I was trying to go home, not stay here.

THIRTEEN

MANN GRABBED A DRINK and met Amie in the bedroom. She was sitting at her vanity desk, straightening her hair. He stood there staring at her. She looked good even when she wasn't dressed up. It finally hit him that his wife was nothing like her. Amie had more going for herself, and that wasn't counting the fact that her body was by far more stacked than his wife's was. If there was a person that he could see himself being with for the rest of his life, it would be her. He walked up behind Amie and kissed the back of her head. "Hey, beautiful, wanna fool around a bit?"

She giggled like a little girl who just received a kiss from her crush. She turned around toward Mann and acted like she was surprised. "I'm trying to do my hair, now leave me alone."

"I'll leave you alone," he said, dropping down to his knees in front of her. Amie was wearing a leopard nightgown that he slowly lifted up to her thighs. Her pussy was on fire and throbbing for attention. She quickly removed it the rest of the way. Her titties were the size of ripe grapefruits, and her nipples were hard as rocks. He tickled each one with the tip of his tongue.

"Damn, you got me so fucking wet," Amie moaned, rubbing her clit and then sticking her finger in his mouth so he could taste her sweet nectar. She took one of her titties and placed it into her mouth and then started sucking on the nipple.

That drove him crazy. Mann stood up and got undressed with the speed of lightning and stood over her as she sat on the chair with her legs spread open. He then ripped off the panties she was wearing, pulling her forward in the chair, so he could go to work on her pussy. Five minutes later, he was bringing her to an orgasm. "This what you wanted, huh?" he whispered.

"How about you shut up and eat," she moaned. "My kids might want to come back home tonight."

Amie let her kids hang out with their friends for the night because she wanted to have some alone time with Mann. They both were having issues with their spouses and decided to move on with each other. She filed for divorce, and he left his pregnant wife and kids and moved into an apartment. People at home and work had plenty to say about it, but neither of them cared. In fact, if you asked Amie if she were single or dating someone, she would say single. She felt like it wasn't anyone's business who she was screwing. She was right though. Her personal life was just that, her personal life. He stood her up and bent her over the vanity table, plowing into her with force causing her to scream out in pleasure and pain. She had him thinking he was killing the pussy, but in all reality, he wasn't that good when it came to sex. What he lacked in bed, he made up for in other ways. That's why she cared so much about him.

"Ssss-awwww," Amie gasped, sucking in air through clenched teeth. Mann slid deeper inside her tight hole, trying to touch her stomach literally. "Ohhh shit, I'm about to cum. Faster, harder." He eagerly accommodated her request as he also felt an orgasm approaching. They both came together to electrifying orgasms, but Amie wasn't done yet. She needed more after being deprived all day. She just wanted him to fuck her until she couldn't be fucked anymore. That's exactly what he tried to do, but was unsuccessful. Instead, he fell asleep after the first nut, and Amie had to please herself until she was satisfied.

~ ~ ~

Every hour someone was wiping down doorknobs and anything else that people touched. Staff and inmates were advised to wear gloves and wash their hands every time they finished doing anything. I was walking Brawny while Stud helped Dan change the linen on the bed of a patient that couldn't move by himself.

Joan was carrying two huge boxes out of the pharmacy when one of them fell out her hand. I rushed over to give her a hand.

"I got it," I told her, picking up the box.

"Thank you! Can you give these to Dan for me?"

I dropped the boxes off at the nurses' station, then continued walking Brawny. I had my tablet on so he could listen to it as he walked. It was just one of the nice things that we usually did for him. In the summer, we would buy him sodas and ice cream from the stand when we took him to the yard. Right now, we couldn't go anywhere because of this COVID-19 shit. When he did go out, he would only walk around the track once before getting tired. In the infirmary, though, he could walk for hours before showing a sign of tiredness.

"Trays are coming," the officer said, making his rounds.

"Here, sit Brawny down while I fill up the utensil box," I said, passing him off to Harris. I walked to the back closet, but it was locked. Just when I was about to call the officer, Jimbo came walking through the door from K1. "Jimbo can you unlock this door for me?"

"Sure!" he said. Once I got the utensils, we served lunch to the patients.

After cleaning up, I was about to go in the room to take a nap, but maintenance came to put up another bunk. My homie Stud was about to come over. We had been talking to Ms. Hart about getting an extra body over, and she finally agreed to do so. Once the bunk bed was in, they measured the opening so they could install a door also. They were pretty quick with the process. Stud moved over that evening, and we were now a five-man crew.

FOURTEEN

MANN AND AMIE LAY in bed watching the news. They were trying to see if there were any new updates on the coronavirus that was spreading throughout the United States. So far it had hit a couple of states. Last night one of the NBA stars was diagnosed with it, causing them to shut down the league temporarily.

"This is so fucked up," Mann said, sipping on a cup of coffee. "They may cancel the league for the rest of the year because of this virus."

"I mean what can you do? Right now, no one is safe unless you simply stay away from everyone. You can't even go out of the country if you wanted to because of flight restrictions."

"That's why I need to get home and make sure my daughter is alright."

"You mean make sure your wife is alright?" Amie said with a disappointed look on her face. "Why the fuck can't you just call them?"

"Look, I can't do this with you right now, okay? You knew what you were getting into when we decided to do this."

"I wish you would have told me that you were married before we fucked. This could have gone totally different, and I wouldn't have caught feelings so fast."

"I told you that I'm working on the details of the divorce. Soon as it's all worked out, we can move on with our lives. You have to trust me. Do you?"

Amie was the type to fall in love quick, so it was no surprise that this was going to happen. All it took was for someone other than her husband to give her the attention she needed, and they had her just like that. She didn't know if she should trust him or not. She loved him and wanted to make things work.

"Yes, I told you before that I trust you. I'm just worried about him dragging this divorce along and trying to keep the house and cars and get custody of the kids," Amie replied, tears coming down her face. "I'm going through the same shit. I hope she don't get greedy also."

Mann had been trying to figure a way out of his relationship with his wife ever since him and Amie started messing around. When some of his coworkers had told him how easy it would be to get in her panties, he thought it would just be a fuck thing and that's all, but it turned into something more. Now he didn't care that she fucked his lieutenant, another sergeant, or any of the other people she bedded. It was all about her right now. He didn't want anybody else to get a shot with her.

"I need to get home and get ready for work. I'll see you when you get there," Mann said, giving her a peck on the cheek. "Just know I only want you to be happy."

"That sounds great, but if you want me to be happy, then I think you should leave me with something to remember you by," Amie said in a seductive manner.

"Let's see what I can do," Mann replied, checking his watch and then walking toward her. "I guess I better hurry up and make you smile for the rest of the day."

"Shut up and fuck me," she laughed, sliding her hand down his chest and his sides as she pressed her hips into his. Amie moved to the edge of the bed and stood up in front of him. She kissed him hard. Her tongue slipped out, parting his mouth, intertwining with his. Mann let her take control. She grabbed his wrist and plunged his hand down her shorts, between her legs, moving aside her panties so that his fingers glided against her pussy. Slippery hot, she sighed heavily in his mouth as she pressed his fingers against her clit, grinding herself against his hand. Mann stroked her pussy until she started to squirm and pant into his mouth. Amie reciprocated the feeling by sticking her hand inside his pants, wrapping her hand around his dick, that was now fully awake, and stroked it nice and slow.

"Shit!" Mann backed up and looked at how beautiful she was. Even without make-up, she still had this glow about her. He didn't understand why she had low self-esteem.

"What?"

"Nothing," he replied.

Amie removed her clothes and leaned back on the mattress, situating her ass and beckoning him to come and get it. Mann's dick was at full attention by now. She grabbed it, positioning it between her legs.

"Just fuck me," she said, urging him on.

His breath was sweet, smelling like mouthwash. As he knelt down in front of her, his fingers opened her up, and he began tonguing her clit. Amie felt herself melting, legs going weak. This was the effect he had over her body, and she loved it. Mann leaned back, pulling her onto the floor with him, and slithered his dick into her wet pussy, smooth and wide. Amie was lost in the exotic world that she would go into every time they had sex. He fucked her deep and hard, his fingers pulling her ass cheeks apart. He slipped one in her ass, sending tiny jolts of pleasure throughout her body, especially her pussy. She pulled herself astride to take him even farther in, gripping as she raised herself to the tip, then bouncing down, feeling every inch of him smooth and hot. Amie lifted her ass and turned toward his legs for the reverse-cowgirl style. The view of her ass drove him crazy. Slow, wet, and warm, Mann rocked her, up and down, teeter-totter, over and over. He fucked her so good that when she came, it flowed out like a water faucet. Now he needed to get his off before he left. He flipped her over on her back, threw her legs up in the air, and pounded away. Amie's breasts bounced up and down with every thrust he gave her.

"I'm about to cum again, baby. Harder, fuck me harder." Mann tried to do just that too. He dug deep into her hole like he was trying to make his dick pop out of her mouth. Amie took everything he could dish out. "I want another baby," she moaned, causing Mann to stop in midstroke. It was like his dick went limp from hearing the words *another baby*! He picked Amie up off of him like she weighed ten pounds.

"What's wrong?" she asked, puzzled. "What did you

just say?"

"I said I want another baby. If you really want to marry me, then put another baby inside me so you can really leave her," Amie stated firmly, not backing down from what she wanted. She was giving him an ultimatum, that either he would agree to or not.

Mann looked at her like she had just given him an STD or something. "This is not the time to be talking about another baby. I told you before that there's too much going on in both of our lives right now. You're still going to school, Amie, and I'm still trying to figure out my next move. I want to move up to management somewhere." Amie was pissed that he was talking to her like that. As much as she wanted to sit there and argue, she knew it wouldn't get anywhere. She was about to say something just so she could have the last word, but his phone began ringing. Mann spoke briefly to the caller, got dressed, and headed out the door without saying a word.

FIFTEEN

MAT WAS THE KILO rover today, so he walked through the infirmary, heading over to K1. Chelsey was sitting in the nurses' station getting ready to do her vitals. Stud was on the phone, and me and Harris were talking to one of the patients.

"Mattie ice, what's going on?" I said when he walked past.

"What's up?"

"What you got mandated today?" Lang asked.

"Naw, I took somebody's mandate. I'll talk to y'all on my way back through," he said, then kept walking. As he was passing the nurses' station, he stopped to speak with Chelsey. "What's up with you? Are you still mad at me?"

"I can't talk right now," she told him as she continued getting ready.

"I wanted to say sorry about the other day, and I want to make it up to you. What time are you taking your break?"

Chelsey looked up at him but didn't say a word. He kept staring at her, waiting to get a response. From the look on his face, she knew that he felt like shit. The more she wanted to ignore him, the more she actually wanted him. She decided to make him earn her forgiveness. "I'm taking my break at 4:15. Meet me downstairs so you can prove how sorry you are."

Mat smirked and headed over to K block without responding. Whenever someone went downstairs after everyone was gone, it was for one reason, and one reason only. She was about to give him some. He couldn't wait to tell his friends if it was good or not. A couple other officers already tasted the goods and said that it wasn't great, but okay. He was about to find out. As soon as he finished counting and took the count sheets to control, he tried to rush back so he could meet her in the boom boom room. He never made it because people kept stopping him. The sergeant wanted him to help with the trash, a stewardess asked him to drop off a tray to the RHU, and other things. He didn't get finished until 5:00.

Chelsey walked downstairs but didn't see anyone. As she approached the dentist office, she thought she heard someone moaning and hurried back up the stairs. When she came through the door, me and Officer Hurts were standing there talking. She had this look on her face that made us stop talking. "I think there's someone downstairs in the dentist office."

"How you know?" Officer Hurts asked.

"'Cause I heard a moaning sound coming from inside," she replied.

We both looked at each other, then back to her. She walked down to the break room. If there was somebody down there, I wanted to see who it was. I told Stud what she said, and we posted up and waited to see who came through those doors. We waited for thirty minutes, but no one came up.

"Wasn't nobody down there," Stud said. "She probably

was hearing things."

We went back to talking and bullshitting around.

~ ~ ~

Jamie and Chad was sitting in the break room eating and talking about someone that had hemorrhoids, when Chelsey walked in. She opened the refrigerator and grabbed her soda, then sat down at the table.

She joined in on the conversation. "I have one, want to see it?" she asked. Neither one of them answered, so she stood up, turned around, and pulled her pants halfway down. Chad turned his head so he couldn't see. Jamie couldn't believe how bold she was.

"What are you doing?" Jamie asked. "I'm trying to show you," she said, then pulled her panties halfway down. Jamie could see how it was poking out of her ass. "I told you I had one, even though it's not all that bad. Chad, don't be shy, you can look at it too."

"Naw, I'm cool. You ladies have fun with that," he replied, walking out the door. Chelsey pulled her clothes up and sat back down. They talked for a few minutes and then she headed back to the nurses' station so the next group of people could go to lunch. "You only have to run an IV in Mush; everyone else is done," Penelope told her as they headed out to lunch.

"Thanks!" She gathered up everything she needed before leaving. I was leaving the clothing closet as she walked by. "Moore, you wanna help me out real quick please?"

"Sure let me give him his clothes and I'll be right there." After giving the patient his clothes, I went to help Chelsey.

I sat on the bed so I could hold his arm while she inserted the needle. She couldn't get it standing up, so she kneeled down between my legs, resting her arm on my thigh. When I felt my dick rising from her touch, I began thinking about something else hoping that it worked. It was hard, but I was able to compose myself.

"Thank you," she said after she was done getting the needle in his arm. I stood up and waited by the door just in case she needed me again. She must have realized that I was staring at her 'cause what she did next was crazy. She bent over, giving me a full view of her assets. No matter what I thought about, it didn't work this time. My shit went straight to attention. Chelsey turned toward me just as I was trying to leave. I know she knew what she was doing because she looked straight at my dick. Later that night, me and my hand had fun, if you know what I mean. I couldn't have the real thing, but I could sure imagine that I did.

SIXTEEN

RENATA AND KIMMY WALKED in together for their shift. Kimmy had the infirmary, and Renata was on K2. She liked working over there anyway because she didn't have to deal with the other nurses. Kimmy was still rather new, so she had yet to experience the back biting and fakeness yet. They would laugh with you, but as soon as you turned your back, you were everything under the sun. Now that all the meds were being distributed on the block, Kimmy only had to deal with the patients inside the infirmary. She looked at it as a relief for the time being. Now she could just concentrate on getting her work done without running an insulin line. Jamie arrived and went in the back with Jimbo so he could brief her on what was going on for the day. This was something the two of them did every day so that they were on the same page.

"Reda had to go home early because she hurt herself trying to change Mush," Jimbo told Jamie as she was filling her water container with ice.

"Did she?"

"Yeah. I wasn't there, so I didn't see it. I took the empty tanks over to the sally port, and when I came back, she was gone."

"No one should have to change him by themselves. He's gonna really hurt somebody one day," Jamie replied, sitting on the edge of the table.

"That's what me and Dan said. Anyway, everyone got their showers except Brawny. He has been in bed all day because he had a high temperature. The doctor believes he has a UTI. They started treating him with an antibiotic. His temp went down a lot from the Tylenol he took."

"Okay!"

They talked for a few more minutes about nothing important, then walked out of the break room. Amy walked into the nurses' station, and Kimmy walked out. Apparently she was switched with Amy because they wanted her to learn C2. Karen and Mick were in the pharmacy today, and Kate was on K1.

"Goodnight," Chris said as she headed out with the other first shift workers.

"Looks like it's Amie and Jamie today," I joked, walking past the office.

"That's right," Jamie replied. She wrote down all the patients' names, then grabbed the machine to take their vitals. Of course Mush was the only one that was wet. He would wait for Jamie to come in, in order to say he had pissed on himself. It was starting to become an everyday occurrence. He could do for himself when she wasn't around, but then it would change when she was.

"Flipper, why do you always wait until she comes in to say you need to be changed? You have all those other nurses sitting in there doing nothing, but you wait for her."

"I didn't have to go then," he said, making up an excuse. "I thought I did, but it was just a fart."

"Well you better get up and use that bathroom when you have to go," she told him. "And you better not shit on yourself."

I helped Jamie change him, and then we sat him in the chair until dinner came. He still had about an hour, but oh well. Oh course he complained that he wanted to lie back down. Nobody cared though. See, this is the thing you have to know about Mush. He was an attention seeker. If he feels like another patient is getting too much attention, he will do whatever he has to to divert that attention to him. One minute he wants a blanket, the next some water. Don't let him know he has commissary. He will beg you for it until everything is gone. Jamie was by far his favorite nurse. It used to be Amie, but most of the time, she worked in the pharmacy, so he never got to see her unless she was walking through. He told me one day that the reason he always waited for her to help him was that he liked the way she touched him. I had to think about it for a minute. Who wouldn't want a female to take care of him? However, that was no excuse for him to use and abuse someone's kindness. I shook my head.

"For the rest of the night, if you need something, ask one of the other nurses. If Jamie wants to come in here and help you with something, then she'll do it," I told him after Jamie left the room. Mush understood what I was telling him, but that didn't mean he was going to do it. He tried his hardest to manipulate people, but it only backfired on him. Everyone was on to his bullshit.

I headed over to the next room to help Jamie fill the pitchers with ice. She didn't need my help because she was already done. Amie walked in with one of the patient's inhalers.

"Hey, how's it going?" she asked the patient. "Wanna sit up so you can take your inhaler?"

"I guess so," he said.

Amie helped him sit up and then gave him to squirts of the spray. She poured some water in his cup and passed it to him. Once she was done, she headed to the Iso rooms to give those patients their meds. Sgt. Bean was on his way over to K1. He started talking to her as she walked into the room. When I came in to check the trash, Mush asked me for a blanket. As I was walking to the closet, the Iso door was ajar. I looked inside, and Sgt. Bean was squeezing Amie's ass. I quickly turned around and walked back down the hall so they didn't see me. That was crazy. He was always talking about how he was happily married, but he was at work trying to fuck the staff. "His

marriage must not be all that happy," I thought to myself as I sat down and waited for them to come out of there. I just didn't want them to know that I saw that. There was nothing that they could do to me if they would have seen me anyway. I just didn't need the twenty-one questions.

"You trying to play cards?" Dom asked. He was one of the patients there. He was in a high-speed chase and crashed. Now he needed a wheelchair to get around in for a while. The nursing staff thought that he was faking, so they had planned to send him back over to K block. They just didn't know when.

"Yeah, we can play after dinner."

"We have to play three men 'cause no one else knows how to play."

"That's cool. Y'all can't beat me anyway. I can play two against one," I joked.

While we were talking, they came out of the room. Sgt. Bean went over to K block, and Amie went back into the nurses' station. I kept my mouth shut about the situation for a long time, but now I'm talking about it. The only person that I said something to before then was Stud. Dinner came and we fed everyone and cleaned up afterward. Once that was done, we sat down and played cards until one of the nurses needed us.

SEVENTEEN

CHELSEY CAME IN A couple days later feeling sick. It was Thursday, and she was scheduled to work the whole weekend. Before she could even get started, she ran back and forth to the bathroom at least three times. It was a strange moment. She took her temperature, then went upstairs to talk to the supervisor. Five minutes later, Dino came running down into the nurses' station, grabbed Chelsey's coat, and then rushed back out and back up the stairs. We were all standing around wondering what happened. Come to find out, one of her friends had tested positive for the COVID-19, and she had recently been around that person. Taking no chances, they escorted her out of the building and told her not to come back until she was tested and had a copy of the results. The prison was taking this coronavirus very seriously. They had set up an emergency protocol procedure just in case a staff member or inmate came in contact with someone who was positive. All the nurses were talking about what happened. A couple even thought she did it so she could have the weekend off. Because of the severity of the situation, they wouldn't know if she was lying or not until she came back.

"They got her ass right up out of here," I said to officer Hurts. "Who knows what she done touched while she was here. We have to spray everything down now."

The nurses were already in the office wiping everything down. Me and Sly started spraying everywhere, while Stud and Harris came behind us wiping the doorknobs, tables, and light switches.

When I was finished, I started talking to Hurts about Chelsey, and he told me that they were talking one day and she told him that she was a squirter. "She said that she squirts all over the place, and it gets everywhere."

"She really told you that?" I thought he was lying about it.

"Yeah, that day we were sitting here talking."

"Wow, she's crazy."

"Yep, that about describes her."

For the rest of the day, Chelsey became the topic of everyone's conversation. Man did they paint her to be this lunatic that needed help. We talked about the time she told me and Kimmy that she was a phone sex operator. She gave us an example of how she used to sound on the phone. Kimmy's face turned red when she started making moaning noises. She told her that it was inappropriate and that she was crazy. I laughed, but thought that she was just misunderstood.

~ ~ ~

That following Wednesday, Chelsey came back to work feeling better than ever. It was like she was never sick. You know that got people talking all kinds of shit. The best part about it, they were no longer talking behind her back. They were saying it while she was within earshot. I was standing by the table when she walked past looking like she wanted to cry again.

She gave me this stare. "I'm about to quit," she whispered, then motioned for me to follow her. She walked down toward the break room, but realized she didn't have any keys yet because she just came in. She stood there, and I could see all over her face how fed up she was.

"What do you mean you're quitting?" I asked.

"I'm tired of these bitches talking shit. They can't keep my name out of their fucking mouths. I just can't work in this kind of environment anymore. I feel like smacking the shit out of one of them right now," Chelsey said, staring at Penelope and Karen, who had walked out of the nurses' station, mumbled something to each other, then walked toward the pharmacy.

"You keep letting them get in between you and your money. Why would you do that? Chelsey, we had this conversation so many times before, but you don't seem to comprehend. What's more important to you, making friends or making money? When you figure that out, you'll be better off."

She knew what I was saying was true, but her pride was interfering with her rational thinking. She was letting peer pressure get the best of her. That's the problem with women, and some men. They let emotions take over their mental. Once that happens, there's no turning back.

"I'm about to go talk to Cherry and Hart," she said, walking away.

"Wait, before you go, I want to tell you something." I felt like it was imperative that I tell her how to channel those emotions.

"What's up?"

"You gotta take all that pain you've been carrying around and let it destroy you from the inside out until everything goes dark. Only then will you be able to see the light and rebuild your soul, and prosper to that person you were born to be. What I'm basically trying to say is, don't let them force you out. If you're going to be a quitter, do it because you want to."

"What are you talking about, you're just an inmate." She shocked me with that.

Here I was trying to help her out, and she was turning on me too. "I may just be an inmate, but I've been through more in life in these last few years than you will see in a lifetime. Don't judge me unless you've walked in my shoes. Nobody here is perfect. The only difference between me and you is the pussy between your legs, and I was caught and you weren't yet. Everyone has done something before, but some just happen to get away with it, while others don't. Do you, though. Since I'm just an inmate, I won't give you any more advice."

I started walking away, but she grabbed my arm. "I'm sorry for lashing out at you. You have been one of the only people that's always been nice to me. Even that one time when we had an exchange of words, you were still kind."

"It's cool. I just want you to fight through all the

adversities you're facing and get at the money, 'cause nobody is going to pay your bills for you. At the end of the day, whatever your mind's made up to do, you're gonna do." On that note, I went back to work, and she went upstairs to talk to Ms. Hart and Cherry.

A few of the nurses had gathered inside the nurses' station and were talking about her. They were saying how she lied about taking the COVID test, amongst other things. I was even starting to think differently about her. I really thought she was bipolar. Officer Hurts came from upstairs laughing and walked over to the office where the nurses were still conversing. "Ida went to use the bathroom, and when she opened the door, Chelsey was sitting in the dark crying," he told them. They all laughed. I heard what he said and shook my head. He was the same person that kept trying to be her friend, but now he was talking about her behind her back. This is how it is in prison, though, so nothing surprises me anymore. They probably even talked about me. The difference is, I didn't give a fuck.

I wanted to see what was going on, so I pretended like I had to go up there to mop. I gathered up everything I needed and carried it up to the second floor. It was dirty as hell, so I wasn't pretending anymore. She was in the office talking to Dino. I swept the hallway, then mopped the floor. She was still in there. Once I finished with the floor, I began sweeping down the stairs. When I heard her telling Dino that it was nice talking to him, I hurried back to the top of the stairs.

She walked through the door. "I'm out of here. This place can kiss my ass," she said, walking down the steps.

"Damn, I'm going to miss you," I told her.

"I'ma miss you too," she replied.

Suddenly Chelsey stopped, turned around, and came back up the stairs. I thought she was about to cause some more ruckus before she left. She stopped in front of me. "Shit, I'm out anyway," she said, then put her arms around me, giving me a hug. Her body was pressed tightly against mine. Even though I was feeling uncomfortable, my dick was saying something totally different.

"Chelsey, what are you doing?" I whispered. My arms were at my side, because I didn't know what to do.

"Shut up! You know you like it," she replied, then reached for my dick.

I jumped back, looking at the door just in case Dino came walking through it. She gave me a look like she wanted to call me a pussy. What she didn't realize was, if I wasn't in prison, I would have given her exactly what she wanted. You know how the saying goes, "Once you go black, you never go back!" Her ass would have been stalking me on some fatal attraction shit. But I couldn't risk it here. I'm trying to make it out unscathed.

"You take care of yourself."

"You do the same," she said, turning around and walking down the stairs. "I'ma hit you up on Facebook, so accept my request when you get out and inbox me a message."

"Aiight!"

EIGHTEEN

THIS CORONAVIRUS HAD THE world in an uproar. People were dropping left and right, and it was only getting worse. Since there was a shortage of nurses and correction officers, a lot of the staff here had been working countless hours of overtime. It was also causing tension between them. Brad was going over his papers so he could go do his med run. Helena was the team leader for the day, and everyone hated it. She was already causing a bunch of problems, and now it was beginning to bother Chad. Because it was the weekend, management was off, so whoever had the most seniority was assigned the team leader position.

We were sitting in the room across from the office watching television when we heard someone getting yelled at. It was Brad yelling at Helena. "You need to watch who the fuck you're talking to. You're not my boss. Maybe if you get off your lazy ass and go do some work instead of hiding in the fucking office, we can all get our fucking jobs done."

"I do my job. I'm the best thing that ever happened to this place," she snapped back.

"Whatever. The best part of you ran down your mother's ass crack." The mouths of all the nurses sitting in the office dropped wide open. No one could believe how he just talked to her. Neither could I, but I was glad that somebody finally told her ass off. For some strange reason, she thought she was better than everyone else. It was about time that she was knocked off that pedestal.

"Come on, Helena, let's go back over to K-block," Chris stated. She was also working a double today. The two of them were good friends. People hated Chris just as much as they hated Helena. They thought that she was a sneaky and conniving bitch. Just because her husband was a lieutenant at another prison and her brother worked here in the maintenance department, she thought her shit didn't stink.

"Y-y-yo, he j-j-j-just cursed her the f-f-f-fuck out," Stud said.

Me, Harris, and Lang kept watching to see if they were going to keep arguing, but they didn't. You can best believe that the CHCA was going to hear about this on Monday. It was just a matter of who was going to be the snitch.

"Good job, Brad," I said as he walked past.

"Yeah, yeah. She thinks she runs the place," he replied.

He headed out to the blocks to do his meds. For the rest of the day, the office vibe was somber. Helena wasn't trying to boss people around anymore. In fact, she stayed away from the infirmary until she was done with everything.

~ ~ ~

"Are you going to take your break now?"

"Yeah, let me finish these notes and I'll be ready."

H and Tiny were about to take their break, but wanted to wait for Karen. She was working a half shift tonight.

Once she finished her notes, they all walked to the staff dining hall to get something to eat. Neither of them ate the food, so they brought snacks from the vending machine. On their way back, H and Karen stopped to check all the patients to see if they were wet. They didn't want to go into the break room and then have to come right out because someone needed to be changed.

"What are you watching?" Karen asked as they checked Brawny's pull-up. He was still dry.

"Oh, this is *Wilding Out* with Nick Cannon," I replied. "He's been asleep all night so far. I'm kind of surprised that he's not wet, considering the amount of water he drank all day."

"Well he's definitely dry," H said as her and Karen covered him back up with the blanket. "If you need us, just come down and tap on the door."

After they finished checking the patients, they headed to the break room to eat and relax. They left the door partially ajar just in case I needed them. The officer came in and asked me for some ice.

"How much do you need?" I asked, grabbing a small trash bag. "Just enough for a pitcher. It's for the guy upstairs in overflow."

George Jefferson was the ten to six officer. The reason everyone called him George Jefferson was because he resembled him. He had the same hair style and everything.

He was a cool dude though. We had plenty of good conversations when we talked. Through him, I kept up on what was happening on the outside to a certain extent. Especially when it came to the latest music. He also kept me in the loop on other things, too, as long as it didn't have anything to do with the prison or the security of the prison. I mean, there were only certain things you could talk about since I was a prisoner.

H gave him the ice, and he needed an extra blanket to take up also. I went down the hall to grab one out of the closet. As I came out, I could hear the nurses in the break room talking. What caught my attention was they were talking about sex. One of them was telling the other two about how bad her husband was in bed and that she was never satisfied. She said she had to use her toys sometimes just to have an orgasm. She was even heard saying that he had a little dick. What I do respect about her was, even though he didn't satisfy her, she never strayed into someone else's bed.

I could never understand that though. Women talk crazy about their men, but they're married to them. Why stay married to someone that you really don't want to be with? Is it for stability? Is it because they can't find someone else? I'm going to find out one day.

Once the talking stopped, I knew they were about to come out. Plus it was time for them to make their rounds. On cue, Karen and Tiny walked out and headed toward the office. They grabbed some gloves and then made their rounds. Looking at them made me think about what I'd heard earlier. I didn't say anything about it. I just smiled and helped them change the patients that needed to be.

Soon as they were finished, H went with Tiny down to the pharmacy to finish getting meds ready. Karen went back to the nurses' station and sat at the computer. Trying to be funny, I decided to mess with her. I walked up and stood by the door.

"Who's coming in to relieve you?"

"Mariana said she was going to be here by three," she replied, only taking her eyes off the monitor to answer my question.

"How's the family? Everything good?"

"Everything's fine." She could feel me staring at her and looked up. She could tell that I knew something because her mood switched up. I noticed it also and started walking away. "Moore come here."

"What's up?" I said, walking back over.

"Why did you ask me how my family was doing? You heard us talking back there, didn't you?"

I tried to play it off, but the smile on my face said it all.

"Oh my God, Moore, you did hear that." Her face turned beat red, and she put her hands over her mouth. It was funny to see how embarrassed she was feeling right now. I gave her this look, assuring her that her secret was safe with me.

"I didn't hear nothing, or see nothing," I told her. "Don't worry about nothing. Whatever y'all was talking about was your business."

"Moore, you better not say anything either," Karen said in a threatening but friendly manner. I got the hint. I went back in the room and continued watching television until I was tired. Once I was tired, I woke Harris up so he could take over. Karen was leaving around the same time. She smiled and said good night. I waved bye to her. As soon as my head hit the pillow, I was out like a light.

NINTEEN

TARA WAS DOING HER morning meds. Harris had told her that Willie had not used the bathroom in days, so she put a little something in his drink. She knew he wouldn't take it regularly, and since he kept asking for juice, that was the perfect opportunity for her to make her move.

"Hey, Willie, here's your drink," she said, passing him the cup. He drank the cup of juice like it was water and then asked for more. Harris gave him another cup of juice, this time without the substance. Now all they had to do was wait until he was ready to erupt. It didn't take long before he was asking someone to take him to the bathroom. Once, twice, three times he used it.

Stud came in and asked him what was wrong. "Willie, Willie, what's up?"

"That fucking bitch drugged me," he said. Everyone burst out laughing.

"Who drugged you, Willie?"

"That nurse," he replied, pointing at Tara when she walked past.

He was the talk of the infirmary for the rest of the day. We kept making fun of him every time he needed to go to the bathroom. It definitely cleaned him out though. While we were messing with him, something was going on over on K1. The porters were refusing to work, so they called the sergeant and unit manager over to find out what was going on. We wanted to know also. It seemed that the K1 nurse was demanding the porters to do something and was being disrespectful about it, so they refused. As a porter, you're only required to do certain things within your job function. Anything over that is just you being helpful. Some of the nurses think you are supposed to go over and beyond. That's not how it works. Besides that, we don't work for the nurses, we assist them. Technically, if we wanted to be petty, we didn't even have to walk and feed Brawny because it was not our job. We did it because we really cared about the patients.

I didn't know the extent of why those guys were refusing to work, but it had to be something if they needed all those people over there. There were four guards, a lieutenant, a sergeant, and Spintack, the unit manager. The reason everyone called him Spintack was that anything you asked him, he would spin you. He'd never done that to me so far (knock on wood), and hopefully he never would. They were over there for about forty-five minutes. Next thing I knew, three people were being moved off the block. All three of them had quit and wanted to go back to a regular block. As they walked through the infirmary, we tried to get the scoop, but they acted like they didn't want to talk. I guess they were scared because they were being escorted by the lieutenant and the sergeant.

When the counselor came through with her friend who was a psychiatrist, Stud asked them to see why those guys quit. She said she didn't know anything about it because she wasn't over there. He asked her to let him know when she came back.

"I'll let you know," she replied.

Later that day, we found out that the nurse was trying to put her job off on them, and they weren't going for it. As usual, the staff was taking up for their coworkers, and they didn't want to do anything about it. That made the three inmates that quit furious, and they decided to leave. Spintack transferred three new workers to A block, which was the new quarantine block for the prison. They had to be over there for fourteen days before they could go over to work. They didn't mind as long as they got paid.

~ ~ ~

"Anyone seen Jamie?" Kimmy asked. Cherry had called down for her to come up and get some papers she needed.

"She's in the Iso room changing Mush," Lang said.

"Why didn't she wait for me? I told her that I was going to help her." Kimmy grabbed a pair of gloves and left the office to assist Jamie.

Since this coronavirus bullshit happened, whenever some-one went out to the hospital, they had to be placed in isolation to be quarantined for two weeks. It sucked because we only had two Iso rooms in the infirmary. Anyone else that went out and came back had to go to the POC upstairs, which was the overflow for the infirmary, or they had to go to the RHU. They had cleared up a whole tier just for isolation cells. Mush had been in the hospital for a week because he was incoherent. After getting out of the ICU unit, he was able to come back to the prison. He had finished his quarantine, and was brought out of the isolation room and into bay 3. Then he needed to go back to the hospital, but was only there for a couple of hours and had to go back in isolation. While Jamie was changing him, one of the rails on the bed broke and fell on her foot.

"Damn it," she yelled.

"What happened?" Kimmy said.

"That rail fell on my toe."

"You okay?"

"I hope so!"

Once they were done changing Mush, they left the room. Jamie was limping, but she wasn't letting on about how bad it felt. When she sat down in the office and pulled off her shoe and sock, her big toe and a little of the area around it was black and blue. It was beginning to swell up also. Brad was sitting at the desk when she was checking her foot.

"Damn, Jamie, what did you do?" he asked.

She told him what happened.

"Hey, Moore, can I get a bag of ice and a towel please?"

I gave him the stuff he asked for, plus a chair so she could prop her leg up. He placed the ice pack on her foot and told her to sit there and let the swelling go down. Cherry came down a few minutes later because she was trying to fill in some overtime slots. When she noticed Jamie's foot, her mouth dropped open. She asked what happened. When she told her how her foot got injured, she went down to the isolation room to see how bad the bed rail was.

"Moore, come here for a minute."

I walked down to the isolation room with her to look at the rail. Even though I wasn't supposed to go in, I did anyway, but I put on a smock. The part that was messed up needed to be welded back on. I tied it up with a couple of shoestrings until someone could come fix it.

"Thank you, Moore. I'm going to put in a work order when I go back upstairs. Can we turn that side of the bed around so nobody tries to pull that rail down?"

"Yeah, but that's the head of the bed. So he won't be able to put that side up as much," I told her.

"That's right."

"I can push that side close to the wall though, and leave just enough space for when they're changing him." She agreed to do it that way. When we were done, she went back to the office to see how Jamie was doing, and I went back over to the table.

~ ~ ~

Later that night Mick had to help Jamie out to her car. He picked her up and carried her like a baby. The whole time his hand was gripping her ass. It was funny to Jamie because she hadn't let another man besides her husband touch her like that since getting married. It was harmless though.

She felt like making him feel uncomfortable. "Did you like touching my ass?" she asked jokingly.

"No!"

"I hope you enjoyed it, 'cause that's as close as you'll ever get to my goodies."

Mick laughed and put her down by her car. He helped her get in and then went back through the Sally port so he could get back to work. The next day Jamie went to the doctors to get it looked at. She still came back to work against the doctor's orders. That's one thing I could say about her: she was one tough lady.

TWENTY

MICK WAS SITTING At home trying to watch a movie and relax. His wife was still at work, and since it was his day off, he was enjoying this down time. Once the movie went off, he picked up his phone and started looking through his Facebook account. There were a lot of people trolling different things. When he checked his inbox, he had four messages. One message stuck out to him. It was a message from Chelsey. He opened it up.

"Hey, how are you doing? How is everyone at work doing? Do you miss me yet? I miss you and a couple other people. Can I come to your house this weekend if you're not busy?"

He thought about the last time he let her stay at his crib. She didn't want to leave. Then she was walking around his house wearing lingerie like she lived there while his wife was in the other room. He couldn't go through that again, so he messaged her back and declined. "Sorry, but I can't do that. My wife don't want no more company."

He sent the message and then checked the rest of his messages. After checking his messages, he posted a couple of pics that him and a couple of his friends took. They all bought motorcycles for the summer. They were planning on going to bike fest if this COVID shit was over by then. Right before he was about to get off of Facebook, Chelsey started liking the pictures he posted. Then she sent him a picture of her in a bikini on all fours. It was an old pic that she had taken when she went overseas.

He stared at the pic for a few minutes, then deleted it. She was becoming a problem, and he needed to do something about it before it got out of hand. He told her to stop sending pics like that or he was going to block her from his page. Reluctantly, she stopped doing it. For the time being, that is. He logged out of Facebook and went into the kitchen to get something to drink.

"Mick," he heard his wife call out. "I'm in here," he answered.

She walked into the kitchen, gave him a kiss, and then went into the room to take a shower and change her clothes. When she was done, the two of them cooked dinner together and then sat down and ate while watching one of her favorite movies. It was a movie on Lifetime called *My Killer Neighbor*. Whatever she wanted, Mick gave her. He was feeling guilty about the picture that Chelsey sent him. Even though he didn't do anything, it was the principle of it. He didn't need the guilt on his conscience, but it was lingering there.

~ ~ ~

Around one o'clock in the morning, Mick received a text message from Chelsey. He was asleep, but his wife wasn't. Thinking that it was his job, she picked up his phone and checked to see who had text him. Her face turned red as she read the message.

"Hey, did I do something wrong? Why won't you reply to any of my messages? You're breaking my heart. How do you like this?"

Chelsey sent him a picture of her in the bathtub. Mick's wife was so mad that she knocked the lamp off the table, waking Mick up out of his sleep. He jumped out of bed, thinking that an intruder was in their home.

"What's wrong?" he asked, looking around the room.

She held up his phone so he could see the picture. "I knew there was a reason I didn't trust that bitch. Why the hell is she sending you naked pictures of her in the fucking bathtub?"

Mick didn't know how to answer that, or if he should answer seeing the look on his wife's face. He held up his arms as if to say, "I don't know." Of course she wasn't trying to hear that. Trying to get to the bottom of it all, she dialed Chelsey's number. It went straight to voicemail.

"She better answer her fucking phone," she said, dialing her number again.

This time she did answer. "So I guess you did like the picture, huh?" Chelsey whispered in a seductive voice. "Should I send a better one for you to jerk off to?"

"And I'll kick your ass myself," Mick's wife snapped. Silence. Chelsey didn't know what to say, so she didn't say anything. Mick stood there silent also.

His wife was about to say something, but then Chelsey spoke. "I'm sorry, I didn't kn . . ."

"Don't even finish that statement. You knew exactly who you sent that text and photo to. You weren't expecting me to be on the other end of this phone. I want you to listen and hear me well. If you don't stop texting my husband, when I see you, I'ma bitch smack you so hard that your grandkids will come out well behaved. Good-fucking-bye," she said, then ended the call.

"I blocked her on Facebook, but I forgot to block her on my phone," Mick stated.

"Well delete it now," she said, passing him his phone. Mick did as he was told. He was so glad that she didn't work with him anymore. For the rest of the night, he slept with one eye open, thinking that his wife was going to hurt him when he went to sleep. He knew he should have told her everything, but he didn't. The next day, he was walking around on eggshells until they sat down and had a long talk. Everything ended up working itself out. Boy was he happy.

TWENTY-ONE

"I CAN COME IN today at two if you need me to," Ly said, talking to his job on the phone.

"Which block you want to work? We have F2 or L and M rover," the lieutenant stated.

"It don't matter to me. Wherever you want to put me, sir, is fine by me," he said, trying to hurry up and get off the phone. He never should have answered it, but he wanted the overtime.

"Okay, see you at two," the lieutenant said, then ended the call.

"Damn you almost got me in trouble, girl," Ly mumbled, holding the back of Kimmy's head as she bobbed it back and forth on his erection. They were at her house, which was only about twenty minutes from the prison, having an intimate encounter. The tension had been building between them for a couple of weeks now, but neither acted on it out of respect for their jobs and the fact that they both were married. What changed all that was puzzling. One minute they were flirting with each other at work, and the next they were in her bedroom, doing the forbidden dance with each other. He raised his hand to her face, moving his fingers down her chin, the column of her throat, her sternum, searing her with his touch, to the first button of her blouse.

"I want to see you," he whispered, and dexterously unhooked the button. He planted a soft kiss on her parted lips. Kimmy was panting and eager, aroused by the potent combination of his forwardness, his raw sexuality, and the gentle touch of his hands.

"Oh my," she panted, feeling his hand on her breast.

"Strip for me," he whispered, his eyes burning a hole through her clothes. Kimmy was only too happy to comply. Not taking her eyes off of his, she slowly undid each button, savoring his scorching gaze. She could see his desire. It was evident on his face and between his legs. Her head game had him turned on so bad that he couldn't wait to undress her.

He began helping her out of her shirt. She let it fall to the floor and reached for the button on her jeans. "Stop," he ordered. "Sit down." She loved the way he took charge. Her husband was nothing like him. She sat on the edge of the bed, and in one fluid movement he was on his knees in front of her, undoing the laces of first one and then the other sneaker, pulling each off, followed by her socks. Ly picked up her left foot and raised it, planting soft kisses on the pad of her big toe, then grazed his teeth against it.

"Ah!" Kimmy moaned as she felt the affect in her groin.

He stood up in one swift move, held his hand out to her, and pulled her up off the bed. "Continue," he said, standing back to watch her do her thing.

Kimmy eased the zipper of her jeans down and hooked her thumbs in the waistband as she sashayed, then slid them down her legs. A smile displayed on Ly's lips, but his eyes remained dark. It made her feel so sexy, knowing how this man was staring at her. She was wearing white lace panties, with a bra to match. After stepping out of her jeans, she stood there like she was modeling lingerie for him. Reaching behind, she unsnapped her bra, sliding the straps down her arms and dropping it on top of her shirt that was now on the floor. Next, she slowly eased her panties down her nice thick legs, letting them fall to her ankles and stepping out of them. Ly looked at her naked body, without saying a word, desire written all over his face. Besides a couple of stretch marks, Kimmy's body was flawless. Ly pulled off his own shirt, followed by his T-shirt, revealing his fake six pack. His shoes and socks followed before he reached for his pants. She helped him pull them off.

"I want you so bad right now," he whispered in her ear, pulling her into his arms, kissing her neck. "And do not let anyone at work know what we're doing, especially Stud and E. We'll never hear the end of it."

"I won't."

His tongue made its way up to her mouth, where it slid inside, entwining with hers as he slowly walked her backward to the bed, gently lowering her onto it. He lay beside her, pinching her nipples. His hungry mouth found one of her breasts and began sucking on it as his skilled fingers caressed and stroked her clitoris. He moved his hand over her hips and buttocks and down her leg to her knee. The whole time, he never removed his mouth from sucking on her breast. With her back to him, he slid deep inside her from behind, his fingers tightening around her hair. He began pumping slow, then sped up the pace. The deeper he went, the more Kimmy liked it. She closed her eyes and absorbed each stroke. His groans of pleasure had her on the brink of explosion. Her insides began to quiver, and Ly felt her tightening up. That made him speed up even more, going faster and harder. She couldn't hold it any longer and let go, exploding just as he also released his sperm.

"Damn, you just wore me out," she said, leaning back

on her pillow.

"You want something to drink?"

"No, I have to be at work by two. I was next up to be mandated. At least they gave me a good post," Ly replied, putting his clothes back on. He knew he just crossed a line that may or may not come back and haunt them. It was a consequence worth enduring though. She was way better than he thought she would be.

Kimmy stayed in bed and watched him as he rushed out the door. Seeing that he didn't even say goodbye, she sent him a text message: "Goodbye to you too! I guess I'll see you at work tomorrow." Ly smiled when he read the text message, then sat his phone down as he rushed home to get his uniform and equipment, trying not to be late. The whole ride to work, he thought about how good she was in bed and hoped that it wouldn't get awkward at work now that they did it.

TWENTY-TWO

AFTER THE ENCOUNTER WITH Mick's wife a couple of days ago, Chelsey deleted him from everything. She wasn't trying to come in between a happy marriage. She had been getting the wrong signal from him, thinking one thing when it was something totally different. She was now staying out of Philadelphia for a while trying to see what job offerings were available. Since there was a high demand for medical staff because of the COVID-19 takeover, she knew there wouldn't be a problem finding employment.

While she was sitting in her hotel room, she decided to see what was happening on Facebook. People were talking about crazy shit. She posted a couple of things on mental health, then started going through her friend requests. She was big on talking about mental health. Some people would have thought she was an expert, the way she talked. There was no surprise that she had about fifteen requests. People would hit her up all the time on here or Instagram. After screening through them, she only accepted five of them, the rest she declined. Suddenly she remembered that she was supposed to do something. She typed a name in the friend finder box. There were two different profiles of him, so she went through the pictures to see which was the latest one. When she found the one she was looking for, she hit the friend request button. "Well maybe he will contact me when he comes home. He looks good on here," she mumbled to herself as she continued to look through his pics. After Chelsey got off of Facebook, she searched for him on Instagram. She typed his name in, and nothing came up. Maybe he used a different name instead of the one he used for Facebook, she thought. She gave up after a couple of tries and headed into the bathroom to take a shower. The water was soothing to her body. It had her feeling good all over. She stepped out of the shower and wrapped a towel around her wet frame.

Chelsey dried off and put on a pair of panties and a T-shirt. She grabbed her laptop and sat on her bed so she could do some job searching. Since she was in Philly instead of her looking for a job, she went on a dating website to see what kind of men Philly had to offer. "He's hot," Chelsey said out loud, looking at some guy that had his shirt off. She read his profile and noticed that he only liked one-night stands. That was right up her alley. She checked to see how far away he was from where she was located. It said three miles. With nothing to do in that big-ass room, and since she was horny, she inboxed him with her number hoping that he called back. An hour went by and he still hadn't hit her back. She dozed off to sleep. Chelsey suddenly woke up two hours later to the sound of her cell phone ringing. When she looked at the screen, it was a number she had never seen before. "Hello."

"Hello, you sent me a message on the dating site. I'm just returning your call," the deep voice said.

Chelsey was wide awake now. She sat up on her bed

and turned the television down some so she could hear his sexy voice. A momentary nervousness kicked in as she just held the phone to her ear. Finally she spoke. "Yeah, I wanted to know if you wanted to come through and take some of this stress away?"

"Just like that, huh? You don't even know if I'm some kind of serial killer or something."

"Are you?" Chelsey asked. When he didn't respond, she took it as if he wasn't trying to chill. "You know what, maybe this was a mistake. Never mind, I'm good." Chelsey pressed end on her cellphone, disconnecting the call.

He called her back a couple of times, but she sent him straight to voicemail. Her pussy was on fire right now with no one there to put it out. She tried playing with herself, but there was nothing better than a hard dick sliding in and out of her love tunnel. She even contemplated calling that dude back.

"Naw, fuck it." She took another shower and stayed in

bed until she finally went to sleep. The next morning, Chelsey woke up feeling fresher than ever. It was time to get back on her grind, and that's exactly what she did. She put in résumés to five different hospitals, and to her surprise, each one of them contacted her within a couple of hours. She set up as many interviews as she could for the day, got dressed, and headed out with the hopes of landing a job.

TWENTY-THREE

AMIE WAS DRESSED IN a pair of leopard shorts, a white T-shirt, and a pair of heels. Her lips were covered with red lipstick, and her nails with red fingernail polish. This was how she dressed even when she wasn't going anywhere. She finally got another day off, so she decided to spend it with her kids. There was a stuffed chicken in the oven baking, and she was making macaroni and cheese with broccoli to go with it. She had a Strawberry Monster drink sitting on the counter. It was the third one in the last hour. They were one of her favorite drinks.

Her son and two of his friends walked in the kitchen. "Hey, Mom, we're going outside to play catch with the football."

"No you're not. You know you can't be out there while this pandemic is going on. You should be glad that I'm letting you have company. Why don't y'all go to your room and play football on your PlayStation until the food is done," she said. "Matter fact, if you want to do something, take the dogs out back."

"I'll be right back," he told his friends. The whole time his friends were standing there while he was talking to his mother, they were gawking over how good she was looking in those shorts. They couldn't keep their eyes off her. That was one of the reasons they liked coming to his house. After she was done cooking, her, her daughter, and her son all sat down and enjoyed dinner together. They haven't been able to spend much time together because she was always working. That's why this time was so important to them as a family.

"Thanks for cooking dinner, Mom," her daughter said, giving her a hug.

"Yeah, this was really good. I'm full now." Amie cleaned up the dishes, and they all went to the living room to watch a movie together. As soon as they were halfway through the movie, she received a text message. Because her phone was on silent, she didn't hear it.

"I'm tired mom, I'm going to bed," her daughter said, heading upstairs to her room.

"It's still early," she replied, looking for her phone.

When Amie picked up her phone to check the time, she noticed that she had two missed texts. One was from her kids' father, and the other was from Mann. She was going through a heated divorce with her soon-to-be ex-husband, so she was reluctant to look at the message. She checked it anyway. He said that his lawyer would be contacting her tomorrow to go over the details of what he was seeking. She knew exactly what that was. He wanted everything, and she wasn't going for it. He would be in for the fight of his life if he thought she was leaving with nothing.

The next message, from Mann, made her smile a bit.

How about a nightcap? Are you free?

As much as she wanted to, Amie texted him back and told him not tonight because she was spending time with the kids. One thing about her, those kids came before anything. She was very protective when it came to her children.

He sent her another message: "Okay, see you at work tomorrow."

Amie didn't text back. She wished that she could have met up with him to get a quickie in. Her vagina was tingling because it needed some attention. She watched another movie with her son before retiring to her bedroom. By then, all she could think about was sleep. Sex was no longer on her mind.

TWENTY-FOUR

IT HAS BEEN TWO months since the governor shut down Pennsylvania. The whole state was under a strict quarantine. The only thing you could do was sit at home eating or sexing. I think a lot of babies were going to be made during this pandemic. As people were leaving this world, new lives were produced.

"What are you watching?" Mindy asked Stud.

Mindy was another agency nurse. Both her and Kimmy were about to turn over and become state. She used to work here before, but then she left to become a supervisor in a nursing home. After it closed down, she decided to come back to the DOC. At first she felt lost, but now she was starting to get back in the swing of things. The only place she hated working was in the infirmary. It made her nervous.

"Naked and Afraid," he replied.

"That's my favorite show. I would love to go on there, it

se-ems fun."

"You wouldn't be scared?" Stud asked her. He was surprised that she wouldn't mind being nude on television.

"No. God blessed us with beautiful bodies, so you should never be scared to show it off."

As they were talking, Jamie walked in. She was about to fill up the patients' water pitchers like she did every day. The show was on commercial, so she didn't know what they were talking about. When it came back on, she smiled.

"*Naked and Afraid*. I would love to be on there," Jamie said. "I wouldn't eat anything, but I would kill all the animals."

"That's crazy, Ms. Mindy just said the same thing. I'm not going on television showing this body off. It's only for my wife to see," Stud said, rubbing his belly like there was a baby inside.

That made all of them laugh. I walked in the room while

they were still talking about it. Jamie was dead serious about going on that show. When they walked out of the room, me and Stud smirked. Sly walked in the bathroom with his stuff for a shower.

"Anyone have to use the bathroom?" Sly asked. "I'm about to go be naked and afraid."

"I'ma go with you," Stud joked.

"That's what I'm afraid of."

That sparked laughter from everyone in the area. Stud never knew what to say out his mouth. I guess that's why he was on medication. He took psychic meds twice a day. So because of that, people really didn't bother him when he said something out of line, unless it was something too disrespectful. "I wa-wa-wa-was just playing with you," Stud replied, then walked over to mess with his favorite patient, Willie.

We were looking for Officer Ly so we could fill up K2's ice buckets, and he was nowhere to be found. I figured he was with Kimmy. Every time she worked, he chased her around the infirmary. All we had to do was find her, and we'd find him. Just then, she came walking through the door from upstairs, and sure enough, he was right behind her. They were giggling and laughing the whole time.

"Yo, when you're finished chasing tail, can we get some ice?"

"What?"

"Nothing! Can we get some ice please?"

Once he was done talking to Kimmy, we walked down to the break room. Stud came with us. You could tell something was going on with him because he was glowing. When he was around her, he looked like a kid in a candy store. She had him on cloud 9. Don't get it fucked up, she was also feeling the same way. Even though they were both married, they enjoyed the little fling they had going. Whenever one of them wasn't here, the other would ask questions about each other. Me and Stud would fill their heads with lies just to see how they would react. Actually, we didn't lie about the whole thing. We took something that they said and added a few lines to spice it up; then we would spoon feed it to them. They soaked it right up. Now we didn't have to spice anything because the seed was planted.

"Damn, my nigga, she got you whipped already," Stud said, messing with him.

"What you talking about?"

"You know damn well what he talking about," I chimed in.

"Stop playing before we stroll your ass in here," Stud joked, getting real close to Ly. "And I'ma grab that thing too."

"I'm out of here." Me and Ly hurried up and got out of there. Stud was acting stupid again. For the rest of the day, we watched Ly chasing Kimmy everywhere she went. Whenever she went in the back isolation room, he was right there. When she went in the break room, so did he. It was just funny to see how those two were acting. I told Stud that they must have had sex. Of course they would deny it to us because we were inmates, but we could tell by their actions.

~ ~ ~

The next day we were looking out the window at the officers changing shift, when we observed Kimmy and Ly walking down the walk holding hands. Coincidence, I think not. It only confirmed what we were already thinking. Of course, everyone who saw it grinded them up when they came in. Even Hurts, who had found out the next day, got his little comments in when he saw Kimmy. "Kimmy and Ly, sitting in the tree K-I-S-S-I-N-G," Hurts said, picking on her. She started blushing, but she never denied anything. The one thing I can honestly say about her is, she has a good heart, and it takes a lot to piss her off. I'm glad that Ms. Hart welcomed her to the team.

TWENTY-FIVE

OFFICER LINDS CAME IN thirty minutes early from being in the truck because he wanted to eat lunch. There were too many people sitting in the staff dining hall, so he didn't want to stay there and eat. Instead he brought his food back to the infirmary with him to eat in the break room. The relieving officer was sitting in the ten to six room talking with another officer. He said that he would be back after he finished eating. As he was heading toward the nurses break room, he spotted someone sitting in the Infection Control Office. It was Becca, one of the nurses. She was sitting at the desk on the computer looking up a book called *Breaking the Chains* by Ernest Morris, because she knew him personally and wanted him to autograph it for her. Officer Linds tapped on the door and then opened it. "What are you doing in here?"

"Trying to stay away from these cranky-ass bitches who seem like their period is on 24/7. Besides, none of them like me."

"You're joking, right?" Linds asked.

"I wish I was. I'm starting to think that they're all jealous of me. I know I'm the only agency, but they don't have to treat me like that. I would never do that to them."

He could see she was serious. He stepped all the way into the office and closed the door. He felt bad that they were treating her like that. Usually he would enjoy the newbies getting hazed, but this time was different. "Don't feed into that, Becca," he said in a comforting voice. He placed his arm around her, bringing her into his body.

Becca could feel his package swelling up on her shoulder. It was making her horny. She reached over and felt it through his pants. Linds backed up a bit. "Is it true that you like to call yourself Chocolate Thunder?" she asked. He laughed and nodded his head. "So how about you show me how you came up with that name?"

"Come with me. I have a spot where we can go if you have time," Linds stated. When she didn't respond, he stuck his hand down her sweater, feeling her breasts that were just enough to cup. She let out a light moan. Becca looked at the clock. She still had about forty-five minutes before she had to be back on C2. She logged out of the computer and got up to leave.

"Where we going?"

"Come on, I'll show you." They went down the back stairs to the basement and into one of the examination rooms. Linds knew that no one would be coming down there because it was the weekend, so they would have all the privacy they needed. Soon as he closed the door, she pushed him up against the wall and began to unhook his belt. Linds started kissing her, at the same time sticking his hand down the back of her scrubs, feeling her ass. It was soft. Once she had his pants unbuckled and unfastened, Becca pulled down her pants along with her panties as quickly as she could. She stepped out of them, leaving them on the floor. Linds sat down in the chair, motioning for her to come sit on his lap. She turned around and backed on top of him, sliding her pussy down on his dick. The head went in, and then she let her weight down so that his dick was unilaterally inclined to fuck.

"Oh God," she said. "You feel good inside me. This is just what I needed."

Linds wrapped both his arms around her and began to kiss her earlobes and her hair. His fingers started pulling up her sweater until he had it at her shoulders. He grabbed her titties and fondled them while she leaned back against his chest. Becca rocked back and forth on his dick. It felt so good to her that she tried to squeeze her own breasts, but he still had a grip on them. "Just ride it, baby," he whispered. "Your shit is so tight and wet. I see why them bitches is jealous now."

"Yeah, that's because this pussy is the bomb, right?" she moaned, feeling her orgasm forming.

One of his hands slid down her soft bare skin and reached for her clit. Linds licked his middle finger and started circling it, causing Becca to move her body faster.

"You sure can take a lot of dick to have such a small body." Becca wanted to laugh at his dick comment, but she was feeling good right now. Even though it was so small, he knew exactly what to do with it. He fiddled with her pussy until he made her cum. She was breathing hard now from how sweet his fingers felt. He kept fingering her while she rode his dick. "I'm about to cum," he said, pulling out. Becca quickly got down on her knees and placed his dick in her mouth. She sucked him until all his semen went down her throat. After sucking him dry, she stood up.

"You think you have one more round in you?"

Without even answering, Linds stood up and picked her up, sitting her on the examining table. He put his hand between her legs and stuck his finger into her pussy. Becca was still all juicy and slippery from the pounding she just took. When he pulled it out, it was covered in her cum. He stuck it in his mouth, sucking it for a while.

"Dee-licious," he said. "This tastes better than a

peppermint. He put his hands out and spread her legs apart. Then he kneeled over her, guiding his dick into the sticky place between her legs. It felt so good that he thought he would bust immediately. The deeper he went, the more her pussy muscles gripped his dick. Her insides began to melt with pleasure. Lind's pounding got faster and harder. Becca opened her legs even more. Suddenly there was a code called over the radio. As much as he didn't want to stop, he didn't want to get in trouble for not responding either. "I have to go," he said, pulling out of her. He fixed his clothes. When he turned and looked at her, she still had her pants off and a finger inside her pussy. Becca decided to finish pleasing herself since he couldn't finish the job.

"You go ahead. I'll finish this myself," she moaned, closing her eyes. Linds was about to leave until he heard the response being cancelled. He quickly whipped his dick back out and stood between Becca's legs. He inserted his dick and started pumping her pussy like he was about to die. She grabbed his ass cheeks, assisting him by moving his body in and out of her. It only took about three more minutes before he was shooting his load again, this time inside her. Becca stood up and felt Lind's hot jism running down the inside of her leg. She walked over to one of the cabinets and pulled out a towel, wiping herself. She passed it to him so he could wipe his dick off. "You came inside me? Are you crazy? You better hope that I don't get pregnant. This is what I get for not using a condom," she said, putting her clothes back on.

Linds fixed his shit also. "You wanted to do this, and now you're mad at me. How do you think I feel? I do have a girl and kid at home."

"You should have thought about that before you stuck your dick in me. I could have pleased myself like I was about to do when you were about to leave."

"You are crazy," Linds said.

They headed back upstairs, and Linds walked over to get his equipment from the relieving officer. Some of the porters were sitting at the table playing cards when Becca took the walk of shame down the hall past them. She could tell that they knew she just got finished doing something, but didn't know what. I was just wiping down all the doorknobs when I heard him telling the officer what he had done. It didn't take a rocket scientist to know who he was talking about. I pretended like I was still cleaning, listening to their conversation. That boom boom room was off the hook in this place. I wished I was an officer for a couple of hours. I had a couple of people in mind to take down there. By time I was done with them, they would be chasing me around this place wanting more.

TWENTY-SIX

WITH THE PRISON STILL on lockdown, everyone was starting to get antsy. There was nothing to do, and the only movement you had was from your bunk to the dayroom or the bathroom. The superintendent ordered a bunch of PlayStation 4s for all the blocks, trying to keep the peace within the institution. Me and my coworkers were still housed over in the infirmary enjoying the AC. Other than that, nothing was going on.

Jamie was just returning from taking temps off the blocks and looked pissed. She went into the nurses' station briefly, then headed to the break room. When she came back into the office, Burnout Barbie was sitting at the desk. She was relieving Kimmy for lunch. I don't know what was said, but suddenly Jamie snapped out on Burnout Barbie. It almost came to the point where I thought they were about to fight. If it wasn't for Penelope just so happening to be in the office at that moment,

Jamie probably would have swung on her. Instead, she went to check on the patients. I could see it all on her face that her blood was boiling.

"Are you okay Ms. J?" I asked her when I came in to help her change Mush.

"No, I wanna knock her dumb ass out. She's lucky Penelope was in the office," she replied.

"After we finish with him, just go sit down for a while and get yourself together. We got this," Stud told her. He had walked in when she was telling me and Lang what almost happened. By the time Jamie was done with changing the patients, she was still mad, but not as much as she was in the beginning. She even went back in the office, but didn't say anything to Burnout Barbie. For the rest of the day, Jamie put whatever animosity she had toward her to the side and did her job. There were a lot of staff that didn't like some of the things that Burnout Barbie did, but they tolerated her because of the workplace.

"Hey, one of you want to run upstairs and grab the

supplies that were left in the hallway?" Officer Hurts said when he came back from making his rounds.

"I got them," Lang replied before any of us could say anything. He was in the bathroom when Hurts asked.

The thing is, I think the reason he always wants to run upstairs all of a sudden is to be nosey, or give up information. Whatever the case may be, he better not let me catch him doing some shady shit. Me and him will definitely have a problem, and it won't be pretty.

~ ~ ~

Officer McRose was late coming in once again because of Officer Ly. He would always take his time going out to relieve her. By time she came in, it would be almost seven. The K rover didn't mind her coming in late, as long as he got to enjoy the AC. Besides that, he liked being around the nurses.

"It's about time," Lang said when she walked in the door.

"What are you talking about, Lang?"

"Nothing." She waved him off and walked inside the bathroom. That was her daily routine. Officer McRose didn't like to go to the bathroom when she was in the truck. She would wait until she came in the building. When she came out, she changed keys with the rover, then made her rounds. She spoke to all the workers and the couple of nurses that were in the office. When she got to the end of the hall, the K-block officer was standing at the door, so she talked to her for a few minutes, then went upstairs. She checked on the overflow patients that were housed in the POC, then headed back downstairs. As soon as she walked through the door, out of nowhere, a snake lunged at her. McRose screamed so loud, then jumped back, dropping her radio and the phone she was carrying. Everyone standing around burst out in laughter. She took a second look at the snake and realized it was fake. "That's not funny."

"Oh hell yeah it was," Captain Fred replied.

Her heart was racing. It took her a couple of minutes to

calm down. Once her heart rate went back to being normal, she threw her hat at Officer Unker. He was the one who had set the whole thing up with the captain. They had been planning it for a while, and finally got her. McRose was easy to scare. They got her at least once a week, but this was by far the best one yet.

"Ms. McRose, can you let me in the back to get some ice?" I asked once I saw that she was finished getting herself together.

"Sure," she replied, walking to the back with me.

"They got you, huh?"

"Moore, I'm going to get them all back one day. I could have had a heart attack. What if I broke the phone or my radio?"

"They would have given you a new one," I told her.

While I was getting the ice, Ms. McRose was talking to Officer G. She had seen McRose standing there and wanted to tell her about the conversation she had with another officer. "She called me last night and asked me if

I could give her a rim job," Officer G said.

As soon as I heard that, the volume on my ears was on full blast. I wanted to hear the whole conversation to see who they were talking about. She didn't say the person's name again.

Then Ms. G started talking about this pool party they were going to this weekend. "It's going to be fun, girl. You should come," G said as I was walking out with the ice.

"Thank you Ms. McRose," I told her, leaving so they could continue their conversation. I heard all I wanted to hear anyway. The only thing I didn't hear was who they were talking about. I knew it was another chick though.

"I don't think I'll be able to make it. I have to stay home with the hubby. He's having his surgery next week, and you know how needy men can get when they're hurt."

"Yeah, they're needier than women, that's for sure."

After talking to Ms. G a little longer, Ms. McRose walked back down to her desk where Officer Unker, and Officer Well were sitting. They were talking about all the new officers they had. Now they didn't have to worry about getting mandated every week. They stayed down there talking until they called the 2130 count. Once she counted and gave them their slips, they left. Ms. McRose talked on the phone until it was time for her to leave.

TWENTY-SEVEN

JAMIE VOLUNTEERED TO COME in on her day off. Since she was on break, she decided to call her husband while she was sitting in the office. He was home watching television. He wanted her to stay home with him, but she told him that she wanted the overtime hours. She knew he had planned to take her out, so she kind of felt bad about it.

"I'll be home early tonight. Maybe we can do something," she told him.

"Like what?"

"Well, it is a full moon tonight, and you know how full moons make my kitty purr," she whispered, looking around, hoping that Kimmy didn't hear her. She didn't know what had gotten into her. She hadn't talked that way to her husband in a long time. I guess you could say that she was feeling frisky tonight.

"I hear you talking, but you're not here yet," he replied.

"Just don't fall asleep, and I'll see you when I get there." As soon as Jamie hung up the phone and looked up, Kimmy was staring at her with a smile on her face. She started waving her hand back and forth.

"I always knew you were a naughty girl," Kimmy joked.

"You heard me?" Jamie asked, leaning back in her chair. Kimmy nodded her head. "I thought that he deserves to be rewarded for putting up with me all these years, and boy do I have a treat for him when I get home." She had to cross her legs because she could feel the juices between her legs heating up. That was how her husband made her feel. She never cheated on him, and hoped that he never cheated on her. Even when the sight of another man made her pussy throb, she never strayed. She would go home and take it out on the man she loved all these years.

"What time are you leaving? You know you don't have to stay here til ten. We are perfectly fine, and Brad will tell you the same thing."

"I know, I'ma leave around nine."

Just then Brad came walking in from taking an ice pack to one of the blocks. He was sweating from it being so hot. He sat down on the trashcan. "I was just talking to one of the officers that was fucking with Chelsey out there. He said she tried to kill herself the other day. They had to admit her to a hospital."

"That don't surprise me at all," Jamie said.

"What hospital's she in?" Kimmy asked.

"He didn't say. He found out through social media. I guess somebody posted it on her Facebook. Whatever, we knew it was just a matter of time before it happened anyway," Brad said, walking to the break room to retrieve his soda from the refrigerator.

~ ~ ~

Two weeks later, Amie was working in the infirmary because Mick didn't want her in the pharmacy with him anymore. I don't know who he said something to, but they granted his request. She was officially out, and it was a question of who was in. The overflow was full because of the whole COVID-19 thing. Amie had gone up to give the patients their medication with Officer McRose. Lang filled up three bags with ice to take up to them. When he got up there, he was about to pass them the ice, but she stopped him. She told him that they couldn't have bags of ice and that in order for them to get it, the doctor would have to put in an order for it. Lang tried to tell her that they were just overflows, but she wasn't trying to hear that. He tossed the bags in the trashcan and headed back downstairs. He told us what happened when he took the ice up, and when she came back down, I tried to explain it to her also. She wasn't understanding what we were trying to tell her. It was like it went in one ear and out the other.

"I'm going to send Dino, Cherry, and Hart an email tomorrow and let them know."

"I don't think you should do that," I warned her.

"I have to cover my own ass," she said.

"Why? You didn't do anything wrong. Don't send that, Amie."

"I'm just going to tell them that I didn't let them get ice in a bag. I'll go up there and get the pitchers and fill them up." I tried to tell her not to email them twice, but it was to no avail. Later that night when she was doing her notes and other things, she sent the email to her bosses. This would start something unexpectedly.

~ ~ ~

The next morning, Dino was checking his emails and ran across the one that Amie sent. After he read it, he called the shift commander to ask him about the procedure. He told him that they couldn't have any ice. He nor Dino knew the real story, and instead of asking, they jumped to their own conclusions, and they were still the wrong ones. The shift commander thought that it was POC inmates instead of overflow. That email sparked a big thing between the nurses, inmate workers, and Amie. The inmate workers were told by the regular officer not to help the nurses with anything other than what was on that paper. The nurses were pissed off at Amie because now they had all this extra work to do. The one who was mad the most was Jamie, because her workload would have really been crazy.

"I can't believe she sent that email," Tara said. "It only made things worse for us. You guys are a big help to us. We wouldn't be able to do everything if it wasn't a joint effort."

"What y'all need to do is just take it out on her and not everyone else," Dan said.

All the six to two workers were talking about it. Even the inmate workers said they weren't doing shit for her if she asked. She really caused an uproar over nothing. Later that day when she came to work, just like they talked about earlier, no one did anything for her. Every time she asked someone to do something, they told her they weren't allowed.

We were all sitting in the room when she came back

from upstairs. She had a pitcher in her hand from one of the patients in the overflow rooms. She walked in to ask us a question. "I have the pitcher. Can one of you put hot water in it and take it up to him?"

"We're not allowed to go up there right now," Stud told her.

"Basically, that email caused a lot of drama, so we're not allowed to do anything that isn't on that paper," I said, pointing to the papers that were now taped to the window. She looked at the papers, then back to me.

"Okay! I'm going to talk to Cherry and see what is going on. I will read that later. Can you at least fill it up and I'll take it up there myself?"

"They don't want us doing anything."

I could see the hurt look on her face. You could tell that she didn't realize how bad she had fucked up. She walked away. We all looked at Hurts, who was standing there smiling. He was the one who posted the papers on the window. A couple of nurses came over to read them and shook their heads. They weren't mad at us; they were mad at Amie. When Jamie heard what happened, she was even madder than the others. Not only would she be running around the hot-ass prison taking temps, but also she would be doing all the shit that we would usually be doing to help them out. Every time one of the patients needed to use the bathroom, instead of us helping them like we used to, we called the nurse. The only thing we could do was assist. Kimmy and Ruth came in to help wash Mush up. When they heard about the whole email thing, they called Amie in to do it. It was so crazy that day. They had to sit there and watch us feed Brawny. That's where I had to draw the line. I couldn't let them take it out on him. He didn't know what the hell was going on, and I refused to subject him to that type of treatment. I didn't care if anyone got mad at me, 'cause they damn sure wasn't going to do anything about it. "I got Brawny."

They looked at me strangely but didn't say anything. I started walking Brawny up and down the hall. Soon Len took over and started walking him. We treated him the same as if none of this was going on. Later that day Me, Stud, and Lang had a meeting with Cherry about the situation. Come to find out, it was a lack of communication on everyone's part. We went back to doing the normal duties, even though some of the workers still didn't want to do anything. The staff was still acting shitty toward Amie. They started talking about how they got her kicked out of the pharmacy and were hoping that she didn't work in the infirmary either. Working in the infirmary has been a gift and a curse for me. What I mean by that is, I've learned a lot on the medical side of things, I received a few certifications to help me when I'm released from prison, and I was able to get enough juice to write this novel. I just want people to see that even though this is a prison, the staff here are still human beings that go through the same struggles of life just like any other person. They are here to do a job and go home to their families just like we want to do when our time is up. As I was finishing up on the last part of this book, I looked up and saw the four new nurses that had come from SCI Retreat. The three women were looking good. There was a lot of chatter already about Amie having some competition now. I found it hilarious. As soon as a new piece of meat comes in, everybody swarms to it to see if they can get it before others. I can't wait to see who gets who.

EPILOGUE

FOR THE LAST FEW days there had been a lot of tension in the infirmary. People were taking sides, and others were staying out of the way. Hurts was giving Amie the silent treatment, and she didn't know why. People were still smiling in her face and shaming her behind her back. Did she deserve it? Maybe! Who are we to judge though? Only God can judge.

"Hey, you," she said, sticking her head in to speak to me.

"What's up?"

"Nothing! How's everything going?"

"It's going," I responded.

"That's a good thing. Remember, don't be a part of the problem, be part of the solution. I'll see you later. I'm working over on D2, E2 today."

"Okay!" She walked off, and I continued what I was doing.

Kimmy was in the infirmary today, and Penelope was the team leader. Mick was in the pharmacy by himself. He got the job done though. I didn't think he would be able to get all those meds poured and have them ready by time they had to be distributed to the blocks. When he walked out pushing the cart and had each block separated accordingly, I was surprised. That meant he was in there doing his thing. I guess you don't need two people to do that, depending on who you are. Stud was playing the game. Lang was running around trying to do everything as usual, and then complained when people kept calling him. Sly was playing in his math book, and Len was walking Brawny. I had just gotten off the phone because it was four o'clock. That's when they go off anyway. Ly was following Kimmy into the isolation room to remove a patient's IV. Once they came out, they went into the break room to talk. I don't know what was said, but when they came out, they were both smiling. I figured Ly was being his usual playful self and Kimmy was eating it all up. She went back in the nurses' station and sat down. Jamie was in there on the computer looking up something.

"That man is crazy," Kimmy said all giggly.

"Who, Ly?" Jamie asked.

She nodded her head.

"Y'all two need to just go ahead and bang and get it over with."

Kimmy looked at her with that we-already-did look. Jamie picked up on it right away. They sat in the office talking until it was time for Kimmy to go to lunch.

We were serving dinner also. Three of the patients were sitting at the table, and the others were eating from their beds. Lang had taken the overflow trays up to them. One of the workers on K1 came to the door, holding up a snack bag for a patient. I went to get it from him.

"Ly, I'm taking this upstairs real quick," I told him.

I walked up the stairs and headed towards the POC. As I was walking I heard a low noise. Not thinking anything of it, I continued walking. There was an office door slightly ajar, and I stopped to say hi. When I peeked inside, she was on the phone. I was about to leave when I saw something that I shouldn't have. Her hand was inside her pants, playing with herself. Suddenly, she looked up and we locked eyes. I tried to move, but my feet weren't working.

"Oh my God, Moore."

THE BETRAYAL WITHIN PT. 2

COMING SOON

To order books, please fill out the order form below:
To order films please go to www.good2gofilms.com

Name:_____

Address:_____

City:_____State:_____Zip Code: _____

Phone:_____

Email:_____

Method of Payment: Check   VISA MASTERCARD

Credit Card#:_ _____

Name as it appears on card: _____

Signature: _____

Item Name	Price	Qty	Amount
48 Hours to Die – Silk White	$14.99		
A Hustler's Dream – Ernest Morris	$14.99		
A Hustler's Dream 2 – Ernest Morris	$14.99		
A Thug's Devotion – J. L. Rose and J. M. McMillon	$14.99		
All Eyes on Tommy Gunz – Warren Holloway	$14.99		
Black Reign – Ernest Morris	$14.99		
Bloody Mayhem Down South – Trayvon Jackson	$14.99		
Bloody Mayhem Down South 2 – Trayvon Jackson	$14.99		
Business Is Business – Silk White	$14.99		
Business Is Business 2 – Silk White	$14.99		
Business Is Business 3 – Silk White	$14.99		
Cash In Cash Out – Assa Raymond Baker	$14.99		
Cash In Cash Out 2 – Assa Raymond Baker	$14.99		
Childhood Sweethearts – Jacob Spears	$14.99		
Childhood Sweethearts 2 – Jacob Spears	$14.99		
Childhood Sweethearts 3 – Jacob Spears	$14.99		
Childhood Sweethearts 4 – Jacob Spears	$14.99		
Connected To The Plug – Dwan Marquis Williams	$14.99		
Connected To The Plug 2 – Dwan Marquis Williams	$14.99		
Connected To The Plug 3 – Dwan Williams	$14.99		
Cost of Betrayal – W.C. Holloway	$14.99		
Cost of Betrayal 2 – W.C. Holloway	$14.99		
Deadly Reunion – Ernest Morris	$14.99		
Dream's Life – Assa Raymond Baker	$14.99		
Flipping Numbers – Ernest Morris	$14.99		
Flipping Numbers 2 – Ernest Morris	$14.99		

Forbidden Pleasure – Ernest Morris	$14.99		
He Loves Me, He Loves You Not – Mychea	$14.99		
He Loves Me, He Loves You Not 2 – Mychea	$14.99		
He Loves Me, He Loves You Not 3 – Mychea	$14.99		
He Loves Me, He Loves You Not 4 – Mychea	$14.99		
He Loves Me, He Loves You Not 5 – Mychea	$14.99		
Killing Signs – Ernest Morris	$14.99		
Killing Signs 2 – Ernest Morris	$14.99		
Kings of the Block – Dwan Willams	$14.99		
Kings of the Block 2 – Dwan Willams	$14.99		
Lord of My Land – Jay Morrison	$14.99		
Lost and Turned Out – Ernest Morris	$14.99		
Love & Dedication – W.C. Holloway	$14.99		
Love Hates Violence – De'Wayne Maris	$14.99		
Love Hates Violence 2 – De'Wayne Maris	$14.99		
Love Hates Violence 3 – De'Wayne Maris	$14.99		
Love Hates Violence 4 – De'Wayne Maris	$14.99		
Married To Da Streets – Silk White	$14.99		
M.E.R.C. – Make Every Rep Count Health and Fitness	$14.99		
Mercenary In Love – J.L. Rose & J.L. Turner	$14.99		
Money Make Me Cum – Ernest Morris	$14.99		
My Besties – Asia Hill	$14.99		
My Besties 2 – Asia Hill	$14.99		
My Besties 3 – Asia Hill	$14.99		
My Besties 4 – Asia Hill	$14.99		
My Boyfriend's Wife – Mychea	$14.99		
My Boyfriend's Wife 2 – Mychea	$14.99		
My Brothers Envy – J. L. Rose	$14.99		
My Brothers Envy 2 – J. L. Rose	$14.99		
Naughty Housewives – Ernest Morris	$14.99		
Naughty Housewives 2 – Ernest Morris	$14.99		
Naughty Housewives 3 – Ernest Morris	$14.99		
Naughty Housewives 4 – Ernest Morris	$14.99		
Never Be The Same – Silk White	$14.99		
Scarred Faces – Assa Raymond Baker	$14.99		

Scarred Knuckles – Assa Raymond Baker	$14.99		
Shades of Revenge – Assa Raymond Baker	$14.99		
Slumped – Jason Brent	$14.99		
Someone's Gonna Get It – Mychea	$14.99		
Stranded – Silk White	$14.99		
Supreme & Justice – Ernest Morris	$14.99		
Supreme & Justice 2 – Ernest Morris	$14.99		
Supreme & Justice 3 – Ernest Morris	$14.99		
Tears of a Hustler – Silk White	$14.99		
Tears of a Hustler 2 – Silk White	$14.99		
Tears of a Hustler 3 – Silk White	$14.99		
Tears of a Hustler 4 – Silk White	$14.99		
Tears of a Hustler 5 – Silk White	$14.99		
Tears of a Hustler 6 – Silk White	$14.99		
The Betrayal Within – Ernest Morris	$14.99		
The Last Love Letter – Warren Holloway	$14.99		
The Last Love Letter 2 – Warren Holloway	$14.99		
The Panty Ripper – Reality Way	$14.99		
The Panty Ripper 3 – Reality Way	$14.99		
The Solution – Jay Morrison	$14.99		
The Teflon Queen – Silk White	$14.99		
The Teflon Queen 2 – Silk White	$14.99		
The Teflon Queen 3 – Silk White	$14.99		
The Teflon Queen 4 – Silk White	$14.99		
The Teflon Queen 5 – Silk White	$14.99		
The Teflon Queen 6 – Silk White	$14.99		
The Vacation – Silk White	$14.99		
Tied To A Boss – J.L. Rose	$14.99		
Tied To A Boss 2 – J.L. Rose	$14.99		
Tied To A Boss 3 – J.L. Rose	$14.99		
Tied To A Boss 4 – J.L. Rose	$14.99		
Tied To A Boss 5 – J.L. Rose	$14.99		
Time Is Money – Silk White	$14.99		
Tomorrow's Not Promised – Robert Torres	$14.99		
Tomorrow's Not Promised 2 – Robert Torres	$14.99		
Two Mask One Heart – Jacob Spears and Trayvon Jackson	$14.99		

Two Mask One Heart 2 – Jacob Spears and Trayvon Jackson	$14.99		
Two Mask One Heart 3 – Jacob Spears and Trayvon Jackson	$14.99		
Wrong Place Wrong Time – Silk White	$14.99		
Young Goonz – Reality Way	$14.99		
Subtotal:			
Tax:			
Shipping (Free) U.S. Media Mail:			
Total:			

Make Checks Payable To: Good2Go Publishing, 7311 W Glass Lane, Laveen, AZ 85339

CPSIA information can be obtained
at www.ICGtesting.com
Printed in the USA
BVHW041847290121
599108BV00029B/359